# The Insomniac Reader

# The Insomniac Reader

## *Stories of the Night*

Kevin Sampsell
*editor*

a *Future Tense* book

Manic D Press
San Francisco

Cover design: Scott Idleman/BLINK
Printed in the United States of America

*Library of Congress Cataloging-in-Publication Data*

The insomniac reader : stories of the night / Kevin Sampsell, editor.
p. cm.
"A future tense book."
ISBN 0-916397-94-7 (trade pbk. original)
1. Night—Fiction. 2. Psychological fiction, American.
I. Sampsell, Kevin.
PS648.N47I57 2005
813'.010833—dc22

2004026465

# CONTENTS

## Now It's Dark

### [An Introduction]

Covered in shadow, silent: things look different at night. People are different at night too. Sometimes desperate, violent, sad. Hunting for adventure, sex, drugs. Cruising around, throwing their bodies recklessly into… anything. Going to bed can feel like giving up to some people.

The lure of the evening world drew me in when I was a teenager. It was a foreign hideaway I wanted to explore, an exciting place that only existed after my parents fell asleep. When friends stayed over we'd try to stay up all night. It would be dark and pin-drop quiet outside. We played out the fantasy where we'd pretend to be the last people alive on earth, walking down the middle of the undriven streets—we owned the town. It didn't matter that we'd probably crash into sleep, exhausted at 8:00 the next morning. What mattered is we stayed up, stalked the town on our bikes, shot baskets on the dark hoops in the park, and invaded abandoned buildings—when everyone else was asleep.

Or so we thought.

There was a perverse pleasure in discovering other sleepless people through the windows of their homes. They'd be watching a late night movie in their underwear, sitting in a recliner. We'd be on the other side of the glass, hidden in the darkness.

One thing about the night scared me during this time: taking out the garbage. My family lived in a small town that had alleys behind the houses and our garbage cans were kept behind our house, about fifty feet from the back door. The neighbor's fence trailed off right by our garbage cans and one of our beat-up old cars was parked nearby, flat-tired and batteryless. I guess I imagined that these things were good places for Bigfoots or aliens or killers to hide around. There was someone who would often walk through the alleys at night, a heavy gym bag slung over his shoulder. I would hear him coughing and kicking at the gravel but I never got up the nerve to find out who it was or what was in the bag. Instead, I would walk cautiously out to the garbage cans, quietly lift the lid, place the garbage in softly, replace the lid, then sprint to the back door before anything could get me.

I never quite shook my fear of that dark alley and its inhabitants but meanwhile I did discover girls. I tried to figure out how their feelings worked at night, as if their hearts softened after the sun sank. Why did sweet compliments spoken at night mean more than in the day?

One girlfriend I had when I was nineteen insisted I keep a blanket in the trunk of my car. We used it on the nights we hopped the fence into the dark playground of a private school. We were never caught. Even if someone had walked right by us, they wouldn't notice our tangled limbs, blacked out from the sycamore trees' shadows.

In my 20s, I often worked the graveyard DJ slot at a radio station. Through a huge window in the control room I'd look out at the city, from this tall building, and wonder if anyone was even listening. Was I supplying the soundtrack for anything? An all-night study session, a police stake-out, a coke binge, a frazzled bartender counting her tips? Perhaps it was just me, again—the last person on earth. Too much time and darkness on my hands.

The night seems so limitless with possibilities, so unpredictable, and fraught with the unknown and hidden. And when you wake up the next morning, there's often that paralyzing moment when you wonder if it was all real or just part of a dream.

Kevin Sampsell
Portland, Oregon

## Everybody Dies in Memphis

**Jonathan Ames**

About two hours after the Tyson-Lewis fight, after the arena had cleared out, after the final press conference, after 20,000 people had collectively shot some kind of cathartic wad of soul-semen and soul-pussy-juice, I found an exit and walked alone across a large, desolate parking lot and up a steep grass embankment. As usual I had fucked up. This was no way to leave the Pyramid Arena. To get back to the world, which was a dangerous dark road underneath a highway, I had to climb a high metal fence. I could have turned back, found a proper exit, but naturally I didn't. I was too lazy to retrace my steps, but not too lazy to climb a fence. In other words, I'm an idiot.

So at the top of the fifteen-foot high fence, as I swung my leg over, my pants, right in the crotch area, got caught in the sharp, rusted wire, which wasn't razor wire, but was just as effective.

Oh, no, Ames, I said to myself, don't fucking rip up your dick, not at 1 a.m. in Memphis.

I couldn't get leverage to unhook my crotch because I couldn't put my hands down on the wire to push off, it would have sliced me up immediately. My fists were in the last safe rung of fencing, and my feet were in holes on either side.

So I was stuck up there, legs straddled, dick near-pierced, feet starting to slip, and a subnormal man in thick glasses and a dirty baseball cap came limping along, carrying a stack of just printed 'Limited Editions' of the local paper, with the headline, "Lewis KO's Tyson in 8." He was some kind of southern homeless man, face contorted and weird from retardation, but the eyes behind the thick glasses were kind and gentle—the disposition of all the Memphians I had met.

"What are you doing on that fence? Are you lost?" he asked.

Lost? "I'm stuck," I said, and looked at him in the silvery light cast by the parking lot below.

"Did you go to the fight?" he asked.

"Yes."

"I'm going to sell these papers!" he said, wanting praise and affirmation from me in his child-like way. He was still searching, as most of us are, retarded or not, for a father to pat him on the back. He looked to be about fifty.

"That's good," I said, and my feet slipped some more. I could feel the loser in me wanting to just let go, give up, get a tetanus gash in my dick or scrotum, and then fall to the ground and break a wrist. But there was the possibility of the dick getting ripped off and me falling to the ground without it and even the loser in me didn't want to see my penis left behind on some rusty wire.

So there I was on the precipice of castrating injury, and not too far away, Denzel Washington was probably doing lines of coke, and the scores of NBA stars who had come to the fight were probably having their impossibly long dicks sucked by one of the thousands of whores who had descended on Memphis, and David Remnick, *The New Yorker* editor, who had come as the thinking-man's observer of the fight, was probably having a nice late dinner and talking to someone intelligent before getting his own dick sucked by one of the thousands of whores. Wait a second, I take that back. I spoke to Remnick briefly. He seemed classy. So he probably wouldn't get his dick sucked, which is my way of saying—I hope I get published in *The New Yorker* someday, Mr. Remnick, should you happen to read this.

Anyway, back to the fence. The subnormal man said, "You want to buy one of my papers?"

"I've got to get down first," I shouted at him.

And then somehow, I did it. I got my leverage toe in a hole, pushed off, the crotch unsnagged, and I shakily scaled down the other side. I bought a paper from the man for two dollars and he staggered away underneath the highway into oblivion, heading in the direction of the beautiful brown Mississippi, which bisects our country like the world's largest septic line. Why the subnormal was going in that direction, away from town where he could sell his papers, I have no idea.

So I, the less retarded of the two of us, though not by much, crossed the road, got out from underneath the highway, and went into the first bar I came across, even though I don't drink anymore. But I was thirsty from my exertions and craved a club soda. The bar was simply a door in the back of a building. There was nothing else around. I was in some urban dead-zone next to the highway. Over the door was a sign that said Discretions and there was a neon beer bottle in a window. I sensed something perverted about the place. I have a good nose for these things. I went in and walked down a hall. At the end of the hall, a little shiny-faced fellow sat on a stool.

"Five dollar cover," he said.

I wasn't sure I wanted to pay five bucks to get into what looked like a dive just to order a club soda, and the shiny fellow saw me hesitate.

"Normally it's forty," he said to lure me, going into his sales pitch, "but because of the fight, we're offering a discount, five dollars, and with that you can become a member of Discretions. You know this is a swingers club, right?"

"No, I didn't know," I said. "What do you mean by 'a swingers club'?"

So I was right, the place was perverted. But I was unsure if 'swinger' meant the same thing in Memphis as it did in New York. Swingers clubs in New York, like Plato's Retreat, have long since expired. Could they possibly still be alive in Tennessee?

Then again, my whole experience for three days in Memphis had left me feeling like I had traveled back in time, as if Elvis's death had permanently frozen the city in the year 1977. So I shouldn't have been shocked to come upon a swingers club.

"It's a bar for couples to meet, and singles, too," the little man on the stool said. "Alternative lifestyles."

So, sure enough, the definition was the same in Memphis as in New York, and while not a swinger, I could definitely fall under the heading of 'alternative,' so I paid my five dollars and went into to the swingers club to swing my dick, to celebrate it not having been severed on that terrible fence.

Well, that was the start of my last night in Tennessee, and I promise I'll return the story to Discretions, to that lovely club, but I'd like to go back to the very beginning of my trip to Memphis, a journey I had taken so I could see a fight, to see something violent and terrible—I hoped—and then to be able to say, "I was there." So, in a way, it was an ego trip, which is always the worse kind of trip to take. It's that old hubris problem. The gods don't like ego, you show too much of it and they stick you on fences and threaten to remove your genitals, metaphorically or otherwise. But enough of that fence, and as I said, let me go back to the beginning, when I first came to Memphis, to this town where Mike Tyson was beaten to a bloody pulp, where Elvis lived and died, where Martin Luther King was shot dead, where the blues were born, and where so much of lurid America seems to have come down the Mississippi and washed up on the banks.

Thursday, June 6, 11:00 a.m.

I take a taxi from the airport and go directly to the Cook Convention Center to pick up my credentials and attend the weigh-ins of the fighters—Lewis at noon, Tyson at three. I plan to check into my sleazy hotel later.

The lobby of the convention center is loaded with cops in riot gear. I give my name and passport and get some kind of wristband. Then a cop frisks me and waves his bomb-detector wand in my armpits and up my ass. No bombs there, except for my sporadic explosive episodes of Irritable Bowel Syndrome with which I destroy toilets and soil the back of my shirt-tails wherever I go.

After being frisked, I go to a room where I get my temporary credentials and have my picture taken for my permanent credentials, which I'll get the next day. Then I head up some stairs to the Media Center where I pick up all sorts of folders and press releases. There are dozens of journalists typing at their laptops, and radio-guys with miniature broadcast stations are talking into microphones. Mounted TVs blast ESPN. I'm in sports-journalist heaven and feel kind of giddy. I can't believe I've pulled this off: press credentials for the Tyson-Lewis fight! A weirdo writer like me. But, also, secretly, I'm a mad closet sports fan. I see Remnick. I see recently deposed *Post* columnist, Wallace Matthews. I'm with the big boys.

I go up another flight of stairs to an enormous hangar-like space, capable of holding rock concerts, political rallies. There are two hundred chairs set up and a stage with a white scale that looks like a cross.

I grab a seat right in the front row. I look around. Leroy Nieman, the famous fight painter, is at the other end of my row. He's drawing a picture of the scale. He has a Dali moustache and is wearing elaborate white and black shoes. An old man with white hair, leaning on a cane stands next to him.

Journalists from all over the world are filling up the chairs. Behind us is another stage with dozens of high-powered cameras with black cannon-like lenses pointing at the scale. So much attention for two men fighting. We've got whole countries fighting. There are huge problems to solve. But I've long since accepted that the world is sick, imbalanced, and lunatic. So while we live with the constant specter of terror, while chunks of polar ice-caps are breaking off, while the Mideast self-immolates, I and thousands of others are gathered in Memphis to see two black men attack one another.

I ask the British photographer sitting next to me, "Excuse me, but do you know who the guy with the white hair and the cane is?"

"That's Bud Shulberg," says the Brit.

Shulberg wrote *On the Waterfront*. He penned the line, 'I could'a been a contender.' No wonder he's at the fight.

"I'm going to try to talk to him and Nieman," I say to the photog.

"Don't bother with Nieman. He's just here to sell paintings. A prostitute."

Suddenly, Nieman does look a little whorish to me. That moustache. Those shoes. I'm very impressionable. I go over to

Shulberg. I hear him say to another reporter, "It could be Shakespearean."

The reporter leaves. "Mr. Shulberg, excuse me," I say, "but did I hear you say you thought the fight could be Shakespearean?"

"I think something out of Shakespeare could happen to Tyson," he says. "There's this violence inside him. I worry that something terrible will happen and he'll come to a terrible end." Shulberg speaks in the sweet, halting tones of an older man.

"Do you think something bad could happen in this fight?"

"I don't know," he says.

"Who do you think is going to win?"

"It's a tough fight to call. Such a mental game. Lewis has to take the fight away from Tyson right away, like Holyfield did. But Tyson doesn't have the jab he used to. He might be naked in there."

I can't think of any more boxing questions, so I say, "I read once about your cross-country trip with F. Scott Fitzgerald."

"Yes, I wrote about that in *The Disenchanted.*"

"The two of you got drunk on a plane and then went to the Winter Carnival at Dartmouth, right?"

"Yes, Scott started out sober. But my father ordered Mums champagne for the flight, and nobody warned me about Scott's problem. Once he started with the champagne, that was it."

"What was Fitzgerald like?"

"He was immensely appealing, awfully likeable. He was interested in you, would really listen. He was interested in people."

I love hearing about Fitzgerald, but then two policemen on motorcycles come roaring into the hangar, followed by three police cars and three white SUVs. Lewis has arrived! Mr. Shulberg and I stop speaking. Lewis emerges from his car—tall, sunglasses, sweatsuit, a Rastafarian hat. He's a physically beautiful human being and I wonder if I'm watching a dead man walking. Lewis is the superior boxer, but Tyson has a lethal punch. If he can land it maybe Lewis dies. That's why we're all here.

Lewis gets on the stage; he's surrounded by his 'team,' his bodyguards—about twenty large black men in powder-blue sweatsuits. SWAT team cops with guns and clubs and biceps line the front of the stage. Lewis's trainer, Emanuelle Steward, undresses Lewis —helps him remove his pants. I once had an amateur fight and my trainer would be intimate like that with me—removing my clothes, rubbing me down. Trainers are like mothers; they're kind to you, sweet, gentle.

Lewis steps on to the scale, just wearing a pair of grey briefs. He's six-foot-five and powerfully built; his hands and arms are enormous; his hair is in braids. I'm not gay, I'm more straight than gay, though I've been known to be crooked, and so I notice the prodigious outline of Lewis's drooping trunk-like cock. How embarrassing for him. Or rather how embarrassing for all us normal-to-underendowed men. Lewis raises his arms in the traditional boxer's pose. White stuff is in his armpits. Cameras flash repeatedly. The announcer calls out, "Two hundred and forty-nine pounds and a quarter."

Lewis steps off the scale. One of his handlers helps him to dress.

1:00 P.M.

After a free lunch provided for the media—pulled pork, coleslaw and beans—I leave the convention center to get some fresh air. At the front of the center, there are six Tyson-protestors—four lesbians and two gay men. They're holding signs that say, "Tyson Opposes Homophobia, Thanks Mike!" and "Thanks Mike for Saying Gay is OK!" I figure their signs are a joke, ironic. I approach one of the lesbians, an overweight girl with nose-piercings and very pretty blue eyes.

"Your sign is a joke, right?" I say.

"Oh, no," she says. "Mike hugged that fellow over there"—she points to a little swishy blonde fellow—"and said, these are his exact words, 'I oppose all anti-gay discrimination.' Everyone is quick to judge him, to give him bad press, so it's important to give him good press when he does something appropriate."

I go to the next lesbian, a waifish girl, cute, also with nose piercings. I'd like to ask her for a date.

"What group are you guys all with?" I ask.

"Some of us are Memphis Area Gay Youth, but also Equality of Tennessee, and that man"—she points to a skinny, scary Edgar Allen Poe-type—"is with Outrage, an organization in London. We just want to support Mike for making a step in the direction of tolerance."

"Have you heard any rumors that Mike Tyson might be bisexual?" I ask. I'm dying to imply that his prison-time may account for his pro-gay sentiments, but I don't want to be rude.

The girl hesitates. Then she says, "Well, from past comments it seems like he is very caught up with anal sex. Some people say he's repressed."

I go over to the little blonde boy who created this whole stir.

"How did Tyson come to hug you?" I ask.

"Well, we were protesting at his training camp, trying to raise consciousness about homophobia in sports and he came out of his car and just hugged me and he said, 'I oppose all...'."

"I know," I say. "So what was it like to be hugged by him?"

This guy is clearly jazzed by the encounter. He's all lit up from within, kind of like Cinderella before midnight. TV cameras are on him, pictures are being snapped.

"I was shocked," he says. "But I wasn't scared. I had to smile and hug him back, being an activist, you know."

If I wasn't such a pansy myself, I'd ask him if he got a hard-on when Tyson's arms went around him, I'm sure he would have happily been Tyson's girl in the pen, but I'm too much of a wimp to be rude to people.

"Are you going to root for him to win?" I ask, which is my polite way of saying, Are you in love with him now that he held you?

"I'm opposed to boxing," he says. "I'm a non-violent person. I just hope neither gets hurt. We're here to raise consciousness. Using anti-gay words in sports, you know, like homo, fag"—he whispers 'homo' and 'fag'—"are just as bad as racist words, like the N word."

"Come on, you're not going to root for him? He hugged you!"

"Well, I hope he doesn't get hurt."

What the hell, he's a sweet kid, and I leave him to be pounced on by ten other eager journalists. It's his big day. Belle of the ball.

3:00 P.M.

Three motorcycle cops, four police cars and five SUVS—Tyson's entrance is more grand than Lewis's. He comes on to the stage and strips himself. His bodyguards, unlike Lewis's, are ragtag, no uniformity of outfit. Tyson's smiling, chewing gum. He throws some punches. He looks to be in good shape. He has enormous pectoral breasts, which must further endear him to the gay community. He jumps onto the scale. He's wearing shorts; you can't tell if his cock is as big as Lewis's. He weighs in at 234.

I had been looking forward to this moment of seeing Tyson in person. But it's a letdown. I read some article recently—don't remember where—which said that scientists have proven that Americans think they have more friends than they actually have because they watch so much TV. Our primitive brains, still using Stone Age operating systems, are designed to think that a face we see often is a friendly face, so if we watch a lot of TV we come to think that these faces, these TV people, these celebrities, are our friends. And that's what I experience when I see Tyson. My brain tells me that I know him already, that he's an old pal. So what's the big deal? Hence, the letdown. So I think that maybe if I could touch him or smell him or be hit by him that would be exciting, but there's no chance I'll get close enough.

A woman journalist behind me, looking at Tyson on the scale, says in a southern drawl, "He's quite a specimen." There's a sexy hint of desire in her voice. I think of Sylvia Plath's lines, "Every woman adores a Fascist,/The boot in the face, the brute..."

9:30 P.M.

I'm on Beale Street, four blocks of blues clubs, neon signs, blaring music, street musicians, Gang Unit police, thousands of people, beer flowing. It's the only street that is alive in Memphis. Everything else is empty 1970s storefronts, abandoned, forgotten.

I don't go into any of the clubs. They're too crowded and there's plenty of free music on the street. I listen to a good blues band playing in a little park. Then I go into a hamburger joint. Sit at the counter. Four sexy, young white-trash girls are at a table. I kind of eye them. This one girl in a halter-top keeps lifting her arms over her head, like she's stretching. When she does it she looks at me, flashing me her oddly super-white, beautiful shaved armpits and sweet breasts.

I order a club soda and french fries. The girl with the pits comes over to me.

"Hi, I'm Jennifer," she says in her southern twang.

"I'm Jonathan."

"Are you drinking?"

"No."

"Why not?"

"Trying not to."

One of her girlfriends joins her, the other two stay at the table.

"Even though you don't drink, can you buy me and my girlfriend a drink? My sister died."

She looks right at me. I can't tell if she's lying.

"I'm sorry about your sister. When did she die?"

"A week ago. I'm out partying to forget, but I tell everybody first thing we meet."

"How'd she die?"

"Car accident. Tractor trailer drove her car off the road... Can you buy us drinks?"

I order drinks for her and her girlfriend. Vodka and cranberry juice. Good for urinary tract infections and getting wasted. The drinks come in big plastic to-go cups. Eight bucks. I'm on a tight budget.

"What religion are you?" she asks me.

"No religion," I lie. I'm afraid to tell her I'm Jewish. I'm in the South, after all.

"I thought maybe you were Catholic," she says.

"Why?"

"Jonathan's a Catholic name... Well, see you." She and her girlfriend suddenly leave me, their drinks in hand. I've been conned. They go out of the restaurant, onto the street. Her two other friends get up to leave. I call one of them over.

"Did your friend's sister die?"

The girl looks a little startled. But she catches on quick, that her girlfriend must have pulled a con. "Yeah, she died."

"How?"

"She was on drugs." She leaves me. I don't know what to believe. Doesn't matter. Those armpits were worth the eight bucks.

10:30 P.M.

I go to the Peabody, which is Memphis's most famous hotel. It's a grand old thing and the lobby, which is a big bar, is packed with an unholy throng of white-trash and black-trash, all gathered for the fight. It's like spring break, but for adults. About a thousand people are jammed into a space the size of a basketball court. The women are all wearing incredibly revealing dresses; the men are either costumed like gangsters or wearing professional sports-team tops and baggy pants.

I'm trying to spot prostitutes, but it's hard to tell the difference between the regular women and the pros. Maybe they're all pros. I do make eye contact with this one lovely woman, who is definitely on the job. She gives me a sweet smile and there's that fake shy look in her eye, as if she and I are in on the same cute joke. But it's not a cute joke. For money, she'll put her legs on my shoulders, we'll pretend to make love, and we'll both feel like hell afterwards. Well, at least I will; I can't speak for her. But she is gorgeous—light brown skin and a figure like a mountain pass in the Tour de France. Then I see her make those same eyes to a pro basketball player, whose name I don't know. He walks over to her, they exchange a few words, and he punches her number into his cell phone. She walks off. The basketball player is then surrounded by four white girls in skimpy dresses.

"You're beautiful!" this one girl says to him. She puts her high-heeled foot next to his. "Your feet are huge!"

FRIDAY, JUNE 7, 11:00 A.M.

I go to Graceland. It's situated on a dreary four-lane highway—Elvis Presley Boulevard—of fried chicken places and gas stations. It must have just been a country road when he bought the house in the '50s.

On line for the tour, several sports journalists nod at me. It's like we're all in Memphis for a long wedding: you get to know people, feel friendly.

Elvis's house blows me away. I never was a huge fan before but now I am. The guy was incredible. Weird. Alive. Driven. Beautiful. I kind of feel like crying. The whole place is one big mausoleum, a wake. He tried so hard for so long—thousands of concerts, thousands of hours in recording studios and on movie sets—no way would he have wanted to die on a toilet at age forty-two from an overdose of pills.

In a museum across from the house, right at the entrance, there's a plaque that says Elvis's heroes were Rudolph Valentino and Captain Marvel, followed by this wild statement: "Everyone shares a common element with Elvis. He encompasses the daring, the familiar, the spiritual, the sexual, the masculine, the androgynous, the eccentric, the traditional, the God-like, the God-fearing, the liberal and the conservative in all of us."

On another plaque, there's a list of Elvis's posthumous accomplishments. Here's one of them: "Guinness World Record—First Live Tour Starring a Performer Who is No Longer Living." I learn that for the last four years, video-concerts of Elvis have been touring around the world to sold-out crowds. And when I look at some pictures of Elvis from his Vegas years, it occurs to me that among the many dreams for himself he made come true, he got to be at the end of his life—when he'd wear his crazy, sparkling capes—his childhood hero: Captain Marvel.

10:00 P.M.

I stagger about the steaming town. Memphis is in complete frenzy now. Everyone is running around, trying to spot someone famous. You hear shrieks and screams up and down the streets when a celebrity like Dikembe Mutumbo or Magic Johnson or a rap star is seen. I come upon twenty black girls all dressed exactly alike—blue terrycloth mini-shorts and mini-tops.

I ask one of the girls, "Are you some kind of group or team?"

"No."

"You just all dress alike?"

"Yeah, we're all friends. We came down from Milwaukee to party."

"Who are you rooting for?"

"Mike Tyson."

Most everyone I ask is rooting for Tyson and predicts that he will win. It's the best story line. People want him to have a second chance. It's projection: we all want second chances. At everything. We all want to prove Fitzgerald wrong that there are no second acts in American life. Larry Merchant, an HBO announcer, said to me earlier in the day, "Tyson's trying to redeem his whole life with this one fight."

I go to the Peabody and it is more packed tonight than last night. I'm hitting that point when you're travelling by yourself and the despair kicks in and you start craving to be with a friend.

But it's nearly impossible to make a friend when you're on the road; hell, it's practically impossible to make friends with my own friends when I'm home in New York City.

SATURDAY, JUNE 8, 11:00 A.M.

I'm in the lobby of my hotel, drinking the bad coffee and waiting for a taxi. A thick, heavyset man with a bald head is also drinking coffee.

"You here for the fight?" he asks me.

"Yes," I say.

"Who do you like?"

"I can't imagine that Tyson can do it. But, maybe, he's got that punch."

"Nah, he won't do it. He's only fought tomato cans the last few years... You need tickets?"

"No, I'm covering it for a newspaper."

"What paper?"

"A New York weekly, *New York Press*."

"I'm from New York, too," he says. "Long Island... So, listen, I got a problem. You know anybody that wants tickets?"

"No," I say.

"Yeah, well, I got ten thousand dollars' worth in my pocket that I have to sell. I was on the streets last night. The Peabody. But nobody with big money is out there. You should write about that. White corporate America didn't come. Three reasons. Turned off by boxing in general. Didn't know if Tyson would do something. And the town. It's a black town."

It hits me that this guy is Mafia. He asks me if he can borrow my cell phone. I give it to him.

"Anthony, no luck," he says into my phone. "I'm going to the airports, hit people when they come off the planes. Then I'll go to the casinos, then the stadium ... right ... I'll call you."

He gives me back my phone. "Listen," he says to me. "You're a writer, right? I have this idea for a sports cartoon. I want to sell it. I called the YES network but they blew me off, fucking bastards."

He tells me the idea; it's actually really good. "So you want to roll up your sleeves," he says after spelling out the concept, "and get to work with me on this? I need a writer for the dialogue."

A Mafia guy is proposing I work with him. I tell him I have no experience with cartoons. He looks at me, disappointed.

"I'm sorry I can't help you," I say. "But it's a really good idea."

His taxi comes. We shake hands goodbye.

2:00 P.M.

I go to the National Civil Rights Museum, which has been built out of the Lorraine Motel where Martin Luther King was shot April 4, 1968. Like Elvis's house, the place has been preserved just as it was—two late '60s cars rest in the parking lot, the original motel sign still stands, and you can look up at the second floor railing where King was killed. Strange: two Kings died in this town. No wonder it has the blues.

There's a modern edition built onto the motel's structure and after walking through galleries portraying the history of Civil

Rights, you come to the room where King spent his last night, which you can look at through a glass partition. His bed is left unmade.

Martin Luther King was only thirty-nine years old when he was murdered. I'm struck by how young he was. Throughout the museum you can hear tapes of his rich, beautiful voice—the speeches and sermons he gave.

There's a plaque outside the motel, beneath his room, like a gravestone. It reads: *They said one to another, 'Behold, here cometh the dreamer... Let us slay him... And we shall see what becomes of his dreams.' —Genesis 37:19-20*

9:45 P.M.

I walk around the floor of the arena. I see Denzel Washington, Magic Johnson, George Foreman, Cuba Gooding, Jr., Matt Dillon, Samuel Jackson, Joe Frazier, Montel Williams, Laila Ali (very beautiful), Morgan Freeman, Val Kilmer, and David Hasselhoff... to name a few. But it's like they're all my friends so I get no thrill out of spotting them. I do get Vince McMahon's autograph for my son, which is nice. Then I approach David Remnick.

"Excuse me, Mr. Remnick," I say. "Can I ask you a few questions? I'm with *New York Press.*"

"Oh, sure."

"Who do you like?"

"Do you want the rationalist answer or the Nietzchean? The rationalist says Lewis. Tyson hasn't had a good fight in years, and Lewis has sufficient skill to keep Tyson away. But he can't afford to make mistakes the way Tyson can, which you can do when you have a punch like Tyson's."

"And the Nietzchean?"

"Tyson."

"Why? Because he's beyond good and evil?"

"Yes, he's crazy."

10:15 P.M.

I've snuck down from my $1,400 seats to $2,500 seats. I'm about a hundred feet from the ring. Tyson enters the arena. The crowd of about 16,000 is on their feet and screaming primal bloody murder. It feels like a massive gang rape is about to take place and we're all the rapists and the victims at the same time. I've smoked crack and the energy in the arena is like five really good hits in a row. My heart is ready to ejaculate itself out of my chest. The place is seething, gladiatorial, rabid.

Lewis comes into the arena and then climbs into the ring. He and Tyson are separated by a phalanx of yellow-shirted security guards; there won't be the traditional touching of gloves. All precautions have been taken so that Tyson doesn't do anything to cost everyone millions of dollars—like throw a punch before the first bell is struck.

Then the first bell is struck. Tyson comes out swinging. Charging like a bull, his squat body launching these missiles which are his arms. Lewis evades and wraps Tyson up, but gets hit a few times. We're all scared. There's mayhem before our eyes. But Lewis is formidable, he lands a few shots, slows Tyson down. He holds Tyson around the neck, which will tire him out. That happened in my little amateur fight. Three minutes race by. The first round is over. Tyson has won the round, but Lewis is not dead. This seems a triumph.

But that round, it turns out, is all Mike Tyson has in him. After that Lewis repeatedly smashes him in the face with his left jab. Tyson's head keeps snapping back violently like something out of a *Rocky* movie. By the third round, I begin to feel quite sorry for Tyson. His face and brain are getting pummeled. He absorbs almost every punch Lewis throws. Every now and then he unleashes a flurry of punches, some life in him wanting to emerge, but by the fifth round, he stops punching and just takes a beating. His face is battered, disfigured.

In the eighth round he takes a shot to his head, which sends his Brooklyn-born brain flying hard against the inside of his own skull. He crumples. Concussed. But he's half-standing. Lewis gives him a shove down to the canvas, so he won't have to hit Tyson any more. Tyson lies there, and puts his hand to his face, like a child covering a wound, ashamed and injured and overwhelmed.

Several minutes later he is standing and being interviewed with Lewis. He reaches up and wipes his own blood off of Lewis's face. It's his best punch of the night: a tender gesture.

1:15 A.M.

I'm in Discretions watching a sexy middle-aged black couple dance. All of the other couples, about five, are unattractive white people in their fifties. Two women, who look like the kind of ladies you see playing bingo, are playfully pinching each other's nipples and laughing. They have their feet in their men's crotches.

Every place in Memphis is packed to the gills, but this joint is nearly empty, except for these aging swingers. What the hell have I stumbled into? There's a sign that says, "No Sex on the Premises."

The black lady on the dance floor hikes up her orange skirt and her man gets behind her and rubs against her beautiful ass. I sip my club soda. They finish their dance. The man comes up to me, "Would you like to dance with my girlfriend?"

"Yes," I say, shocked.

She gives me the same treatment. Lifts that orange skirt. She's in her late forties but hot. She's wearing a thong and has an ass like two halves of a bowling ball. Life is good sometimes. I figure her boyfriend likes to watch. She treats me very nicely. I do worry that I dance like a white boy. But I am a white boy. The dance comes to an end. I thank her and buy the two of them drinks. There's no invitation to come home with them, but I'm not hurt. I get the hell out of there. I have to find a taxi, get to the motel, pack up and catch a 5:30 a.m. plane.

I walk for two hours: no taxis are free. Plenty of hookers on the street are free, but not really free. Finally, I get a cab. The driver says to me, "I've been working 24 hours and I'm not stopping. We may never see something like this again in Memphis."

"I think you're right," I say, and I look out the window to the black morning sky, but if I were being poetic, I'd say it was dark blue.

## No Fear

### Todd Pruzan

It's him. No question. There's an orange twilight haze settling on North Highland, full of red brake lights and cyclists' blinkers, so I nearly miss him sauntering through the shadows past my car, with his olive Nike bag slung over his shoulder and a ski cap on his head—black, No Fear. A ski cap in the middle of September. Nice. And in the few seconds of white space between "I Want You (She's So Heavy)" and "Here Comes the Sun," I watch Caleb turn into himself. Holy mother of God.

It was like this. Half an hour ago, Mom called for the third time today. First was to see if I'd talked to Caleb—as though I'd ever just picked up the phone and said, 'Hey Caleb, what's up, how's it going,' which makes me think she truly has no idea who her sons are. Or maybe she's just optimistic in a way only Prozac might permit. An hour later, she called again to say she thought Caleb was in trouble. I didn't bite. Finally, when I was trying to decide whether to dress up or down, there she was again. Mom!

"Aaron," she whispered, "the campus police just called." I swallowed. "They say they've been looking since Thursday and they can't find him. The police." Frantic, like back when I was in high school and she couldn't control him.

"The campus police," I corrected her. "Big difference." I was thinking mostly of the time junior year they busted me with weed outside the library, and my friends stood around jeering them while I grinned, and all of us knew nobody was gonna break my balls because this was a private university. But my mom's voice had a catch in it. So I wondered: does Caleb pose a threat to his community?

"They're just rent-a-cops, Mom," I said, knowing my voice sounded taut. "They can't make an arrest. They can't fire weapons. Nothing they say is legally binding—"

"But, Aaron, there's a girl, she says Caleb—" In the mirror, my face was flushing. Mom couldn't bring herself to utter the accusation, so she whispered: "—attacked her."

I nicked a little ribbon into my neck—"Shit!"—and put the phone on the sink. I tore a piece of toilet paper and pressed. I could hear her yammer through the shaving cream on the receiver. I picked it up again.

"Mom, Mom," I said. Yelling now. "What is it you think I'm supposed to do?" One shaking hand with the phone, the other with the razor. "I can't do anything. I'm in Atlanta—"

"I talked to the roommate. The roommate hasn't seen him. No idea where he is. The student newspaper wrote an article yesterday." She sighed. "I mean they didn't give his name, but they said this girl was in the hospital—the student hospital, I mean—"

"Mom," I said. "Look, this is really not a good time. I'm running out the door." I snuck a drag—I heard her sneak one, too. "I don't know, I don't know."

"Aaron."

"If he calls, or if the cops call—"

"Aaron. Stop it."

Suddenly, a lightbulb: "Did he maybe go to Dad's?"

I could hear her laugh, once, without smiling. "That'll be the day."

"Look. I'll call you, okay? If I hear from him. Which I won't." I put the cigarette down and rummaged around in the bathroom drawer, snatched the little box, shook a pair of condoms into my palm. "I doubt he even has my number."

"He does," she said.

"What?!" I yelped. "Who gave him my number?" Then her deep sigh. Once per phone call. "I love you," I said. "I gotta run."

My window was open, full of soft perfumed trees and car alarms. I dabbed at my neck. Still a prick of blood. When did all my shirts get so tight around my belly? Shit. When the phone rang a fourth time, I sucked the rest of the cigarette and ate an Altoid and locked the door without answering.

Now, at the stoplight, I finally see what she was talking about. Through my windshield, he looks different from three months ago—his red knobhead's now a floppy, almost friendly haircut, and his body's got some new ropy muscle, after what I'd guess was a summer of protein drinks and free weights and steroids. But it's his walk—like a state trooper toward an SUV with smoked windows—that makes me do a double-take, like some Bugs Bunny dupe. There'd be a mouthful of carrot juice sprayed across my windshield.

First, I'm thinking, C'mon, man, Caleb's in Massachusetts! But I keep watching the guy walk away from my Subaru, and he refuses to do the right thing, to melt into a stranger. And he's with someone, a skinny jumpy guy in long sleeves who leads him through the space between the gas station and the minimart. The driver behind me honks, a Navigator with his lights blinding my mirror, and I lurch, nearly kissing the bumper in front of me.

The thing with Melanie started when one of the girls at her table asked me, "What's tonight's fish?" They seemed kind of like uptight Buckhead types, like maybe they were waiting for me to annoy them or mess up so they could call over the manager. So to be funny, I frowned and pinched my fingers and said, "Tonight's fish is Trey Anastasio, madame." There was this pause, and two of them burst out laughing, and the one who asked the question was like, "Wait... what?" And the fourth girl lowered her chin and looked over the top of her imaginary glasses at me with her mouth bunched into a tight blossom. Stud in her button nose, arch in her eyebrow. And that, it turns out, was Melanie.

I brought them steamed vegetables and brown rice, grilled mango-Texmati salmon, ginger-cilantro chicken breast—and, for Melanie, Bayou chili with extra cheddar, extra onions, extra sour cream, extra extra. Three of them giggled every time I walked past their table, but Melanie stuck her lip out and jerked her head into a nod.

In the kitchen, Lisa, my manager, gave me this queer smile. She's black and she's so hot—I wouldn't stand a chance, but she's totally cool with me.

She says, "Dude. Which table?"

"Eighteen," I said.

She nodded once and pushed through a swinging door with a pitcher of iced tea and came back half a minute later and said, "Cat glasses."

"Nope," I said. "Nose ring."

Lisa did her shocked-mime face. "Huh! So get her number," she said, pinching my gut. I flinched and pushed her hand away.

"'Cause if you don't, Aaron—I swear that I will rag on you until the day you die."

So, whatever. I just did it. I'd never done that before: "Don't leave without our card," I said to them when I handed them the change, minus the four drinks I'd accidentally-on-purpose left off the tab. Melanie's card had my home number on it. My hands fidgeted so hard I had to stuff them in my pockets, until Lisa high-fived me in the kitchen. And damn if it didn't work.

Melanie's call woke me the next morning: "Hey, what about dessert or coffee?"

I hadn't had a serious girlfriend in a while—not since senior year, I guess—but I've come to rely on the third date. If you get to the third date, I think, it could get serious. The first one, we got omelets in Buckhead on a Saturday morning, then went to the High Museum, and I got a hug goodbye many hours later. The second time, we had beers at Manuel's, watching the Braves on TV.

Melanie's from Dallas, and she's someone who enjoys stuff, who doesn't give a shit about guys who wear polo shirts or vacuum their carpets. "My whole day, during the day—I mean, the lab is so uptight," she said.

"The people? Or the hygiene, or what?"

"Both! Everything!" She snatched a cigarette from the pack I was apparently sharing. "It's like, what do I care if there's paramecia crawling around your disgusting bathroom?" Leaning closer: "Which there are," and turning her bottle upside-down to her lips.

Then, pulling me closer, and hiccuping and laughing. And then, all that beer and Marlboros on her tongue—I haven't stopped thinking about it. So soft. Her skin. The place is basically just a roadhouse with a gravel parking lot, but the guy's cool—he put two more Red Bricks down on coasters without us even asking, and then turned around before I could get embarrassed. So we kept kissing, and he never charged us. Like a movie. And then we walked back to her place and kissed for hours on this couch in her kitchen that smelled like it had old hamburgers stuffed in the cushions. The whole time, we could feel her roommates' feet, over and over, creaking down the steps, pausing at the bottom, and then creaking back up.

I didn't know when we'd hang again; her hours at the lab are insane. But on Wednesday night, when I was off work, she called me from work.

"Hey, Aaron, you got a Walkman that gets FM?"

"Course I do," I said. "You need it tonight?" I was already getting my sneakers on when she said she didn't need it—it was for this thing Saturday night, Enjoy the Silence, this monthly rave that moves around Atlanta and was going to be in this warehouse in Cabbagetown that week.

"This DJ comes and spins on a low-watt pirate radio station, and everyone shows up with headphones and tunes to the same frequency and dances around with no music playing out loud. It's so wild. The cops kept busting them for noise, but now he does it every month. Doesn't it sound cool? Everyone dancing and laughing in this rave, in total silence?"

I don't know how she finds out about stuff like that, but I was up for it, because it was going to be the third date, and that's tonight, and now I'm nervous as hell and my brain's humming because tonight has to end at some point, at my house or hers.

And now fucking Caleb shows up, wandering around Atlanta with some pothead. And I'm wrecked. Oh my God. Did he actually do it? Is Caleb a, a... rapist? Because if he is... oh my God. Do I call the cops on him?

There's a spot right in front of the listing little bungalow where Melanie and the three other Table 18 girls live, with their rented, broken-down porch getting choked to death by kudzu. At the front door, the motion headlight goes on, and I nearly drop the wet bottle of Sauvignon Blanc on the porch. I see Melanie get up from the kitchen at the end of the hall, and she searches me as she opens the screen door.

"Aaron," she says, and laughs. "You crash your little Subaru? C'mere, babe, you're just about as white as a dogwood tree."

Mustard-colored blouse, olive painter's jeans, a pair of headphones snaking up from her thigh pocket: for a second, I almost forget that Caleb's out there on North Highland tonight. My mind screams at me—I clench my eyes—whenever I accidentally think of him on a filthy smoky couch in the dim corner of a frat house, with his fat, blank face staring down at some blonde girl crying underneath him, trying to push away his stubbornly insistent body while he doesn't even bother to laugh.

I wonder if he did it.

Shit. I wonder: does he have my address?

It's a decent question, how a boy five years younger than me and who I see maybe once every two years could fill me with the kind of dread that drains my face. Melanie's hardly the first person who's ever asked me. The fireflies are swimming around when we decide to go walk over to the Coca-Cola Commons in the indigo dark with the wine and sit under a tree and make out before we go to Enjoy the Silence. And on the way, I tell her about how I think I saw Caleb, and once we sit down, I twist the corkscrew into the brown paper bag. I don't tell Melanie about the girl in the hospital at Caleb's school. Instead, I start telling her about our old dog, Sophie.

"She was a sheepdog, bigger than me until I reached third grade, and she looked and smelled exactly like a dirty mop. She slept on my bed—a godsend in an ice storm, though I wouldn't part with her furry heat even during a still Berkshires summer. My birthday is in August. School usually started a week later, so I never enjoyed it as much as I should have. Dad had finally moved to Boston for good the summer between seventh and eighth grade—the house was still full of his stuff—and he came home for my party, so he could take me and Chris, Jamie, Carl, and Tim Ting out to see *Die Hard*. I'd waited all summer for it to show up in town. My friends had seen it already, on vacation in Nantucket, or in New York. But it was my birthday.

"Caleb wasn't allowed with us, which was fine with me. He was pretty wound-up, seeing my Dad again, and Mom told him we were all seeing a movie for big kids, and he wouldn't like it, so he had to stay and help her set up the barbecue in the backyard. I don't remember him getting upset. Or maybe I was just figuring out right then that when he got mad, instead of screaming and throwing fits, Caleb would just do this thing where he stood there silently with a tight face, creased and quiet. I'd never seen him do it before. So it didn't scare the living shit out of me yet.

"When Dad brought us all home from the movie, Mom was frantic, and she and my Dad had a hurried conference—probably the first time all summer they'd talked more than 30 seconds—and then he went running and I heard the car start up and the tires squeal, and then the sound of the engine returned two minutes later. My friends went to the backyard, and they watched me for a clue while we slapped a volleyball around the net Mom and Caleb had set up.

"Caleb wasn't around. Neither was Sophie. But he was in his room, sitting on his bed in the gathering dusk, and my Mom and Dad were running back and forth, poking flashlight beams into the yard, the woods. Soon it was blue, then purple, and Dad came and turned the grill off. They rummaged in the garage for flashlights, and Caleb wouldn't leave his room. Chris and Tim Ting went home. Then Jamie. Then Carl.

"After Mom found Sophie the next morning, covered in dead leaves and looking more sorrowful than accusatory, my Dad drove off again, his clothes creased after his night on the leather couch in the den. And I spent the day avenging my ruined birthday, kicking the wall over and over, trying to put a hole between Caleb and me with the heels of my Colorados until Mom wrenched my locked door open and threatened to ground me for twice as long as Caleb."

"So you're the one who got busted," Melanie says. I shrug. She's circling her index finger on my palm. The bottle sits between us in the paper bag. I lift it and swallow.

Melanie sighs. "Sucks being the oldest."

"Yeah, I know," I say. "But wait." I hand the bottle over. Melanie blows cigarette smoke to the side and takes the bottle by the neck.

"Things got bad. Whenever Tim Ting or Carl came by to shoot hoops in the driveway, I'd instruct them to ignore Caleb if he tried to join in. If we did let him play, I'd make sure he got in my way so I could knock him over like a 50-pound bag of Ralston Purina. Once, on a Friday, right after the start of eighth grade, he slapped for the ball and I checked him so hard he skidded on the driveway, wiping the skin off his palms and knees. My guilt was instant, sharp—I reached for him—but then I caught myself and stood straight. The ball skittered into the grass. Caleb picked himself up and stared at me. Then Tim Ting laughed, 'Weird! He doesn't even cry! He's like a little robot!' And I decided I didn't feel a thing.

"Caleb went inside, and we started shooting hoops again. And when we heard glass breaking inside the house, things ripping, thuds pounding the floor, Tim Ting froze with the ball, his eyebrows up. I laughed, 'Someone's cleaning his room tonight'.

"To this day, I don't know why it never occurred to me that Caleb had crossed the forbidden line into my room, where he wasn't allowed without my permission. But I could hardly catch my breath when I stood in my doorway to take in the carnage. My globe was peeled like a half-eaten orange, my bottle collection from around the world shattered, cassettes broken and tape strewn like brown streamers, books and magazines like the end of a parade route. He'd given up on Jocko, my teddy bear, but his bloody palm prints were all over him, on my pillow, my lamp, my walls. He hadn't overlooked a thing. And an hour later, when Mom came home, she found me still pounding on his locked bedroom door, sobbing, screaming, hoarse.

"Mom made us both visit a therapist once a week—same woman, different days—and once in a while, she threatened Caleb with a special school, some place in the woods that had turned a neighbor's boy, Ramsey, from a schoolyard bully into a considerate, newspaper-tossing, driveway-shoveling citizen. But I didn't know how serious she was until a freezing night when she brought me home late after school, after our team's last game of the season."

Melanie's hand tightens. She never turns her face from mine, even when I move the bottle further into the shadows after I see an Emory security jeep roll by.

"I'd had a few good lay-ups that day, but we got edged out. So I was already grouchy when I came in with both arms full of groceries and wondered why Sophie hadn't come through the door to the kitchen to trip me up. She wasn't up in my room either. I was changing into a dry shirt and jeans when I heard the sliding door in the kitchen open, and then Mom screaming. I opened the door, and Caleb rushed up the stairs, pushing me against the wall, and slammed his door shut.

"I jumped three stairs at a time and raced to the kitchen—a tipped-over brown bag on the table, a bottle of Italian dressing broken on the linoleum. Whimpering. Mom on her knees, soles of her sneakers facing me, her head down, saying, 'Aaron... get the blankets, Aaron.' I asked how many, and she said, 'All of them. Just get them.'

"Then I saw she wasn't crying, Sophie was doing all the whimpering. Covered in ice, icicles: her fur a sheet of them, stalactites, her eyes clenched shut, her breath shallow. Off to the side of the patio, in a new lake of ice, the garden hose was still pumping out freezing water."

Melanie sits upright now, cross-legged, with both palms over her mouth.

"Smelly, scratchy army blankets, four of them. Convulsions. Mom making a couple of desperate calls, then scooping up the dog and running into the garage and starting the car. Tim Ting's mom fixing Caleb and me dinner in our kitchen, sandwiches cut incorrectly, with orange juice instead of milk.

"Caleb never came out of his room. I sat in the dark, shaking, waiting for Mom to come home after midnight with Sophie. And, of course, when she returned, half-asleep, Sophie wasn't with her."

"Oh my God," Melanie says. Her cigarette is a rod of ash, beyond what I assumed gravity would permit, but I guess she's an expert.

"Sorry," I say. "I don't mean to freak you out or anything."

She shakes her head. "Aaron," she says. "So what did you do?"

"What did I do..." I say. "The next day I couldn't talk or eat or breathe right, so I just ditched school and sat in the woods snapping twigs and wiping my face on my sleeves. I think Mom must've thought I was going to hurt Caleb—and she was right, I definitely would've tried—so she made me stay with Tim Ting that night, until Dad could drive out from Boston on Saturday so I could stay with him and my grandparents until after the New Year. I came home, and Mom had left me a pile of Christmas presents in my room, but Sophie was still gone. By then, Caleb was at the tiny school somewhere in the woods in the White Mountains, somewhere where you got graded on posture and how fast you could help your schoolmates climb bare pine walls on ropes.

"Three years ago, the end of sophomore year, I took an 8 a.m. macroeconomics final and caught a 10:30 bus to New Hampshire to meet my parents and watch Caleb and 15 other sly, reserved 14-year-olds get diplomas before their huge, awkward families. The school had put rows of steel folding chairs in the grass. The ground was wet and spongy from a morning rainstorm, and my chair kept leaning over. After the headmaster's talk, the families had lunch at damp wooden picnic tables. Dad and Sharon and their baby Steven at one end, me and Mom at the other. Caleb in the middle, taller than me now. Quiet, gentle.

"This was before Caleb would start high school back at home, scaring me away in the summers when I was home from college. Mom made sure she had to be at the office seven nights a week, and the driveway would fill with rusty Jeeps and pickups, and Caleb's huge fat football buddies would drink six, eight, ten cans of beer and pass out on the backyard patio. Other nights, I'd come home and hear the bedsprings working behind Caleb's door, so I'd go sit downstairs watching ESPN, smoking, waiting, and then these girls I'd never seen before would wander downstairs in Caleb's T-shirts and boxers to get something out of the fridge, while Wu Tang Clan and smoke drifted from Caleb's room. The girls never introduced themselves—I never knew who they were—but I don't remember seeing anyone more than once. Maybe twice. He probably did his whole class. In the mornings, he'd be downstairs eating bananas, reading the sports section, like nothing had happened. I'd never brought a girl home in my life."

"Wow," Melanie says, and seems to think about this for a minute. "So, I mean, did you ever ask him—"

"No," I say. "I didn't give a shit." Although what I mean is, I didn't want to know.

"But this was then. Graduation day at Caleb's Mountain School for Wayward Sons Who Scare Their Families to Death. Mom nudged me, her eyes glistening, and I said, 'Hey, Caleb,' and he and I had our first handshake in six years. We talked about junior high in the New Hampshire woods and college in Massachusetts, their relative merits and drawbacks. We smiled at each other for Dad's photo, arms over shoulders, looking like brothers. Caleb said something I don't remember that made me assume I was supposed to laugh and feel grateful that we were normal again."

Melanie runs her finger around and around on my palm. She's quiet for a minute, two minutes, and then she says, "Will you show me the picture?"

I don't say anything. She leans forward and puts her arms over my shoulders, and we kiss, and we sit there like that. People walk by, fast, on their way to dorms and frat houses, laughing in goofball voices.

"So he's down here now," she says.

"So he's down here now," I say, and laugh. "Looking for me. Who knows why."

"You think there's something serious?"

"I think he might have... maybe hurt some girl."

"But, Aaron, you don't know that."

"No, but the cops want to talk to him," I say. "I mean, the campus cops."

"But we don't know," she says.

We sit. The bottle is empty. We tip it back and forth at each other, never letting it fall, until finally she misses and slaps the air and it totters and falls, pointing right at her.

Her keys are gone. We stand on her porch, and she pats her pockets and her shoulders droop and she curses and laughs at the same time.

"Did you leave them inside?" I ask.

She holds up one finger and shakes her head, pacing, and says, "Fuck, I think they fell out at Emory." We try ringing the doorbell a couple times, but it's 10 o'clock, and the rest of Table 18 is out somewhere in Little Five Points drinking blueberry margaritas, so they're going to be hours.

"Well, we could go back and look," I say.

Ten minutes later and we're sitting beneath the trees by the Commons, testing out each one to see if we can remember where we were. Here? Or by that tree right behind and to the left? We decide on one and crawl around it. Nothing. People walk by. Nobody figures out what we're doing, or offers to help us out.

I jump up, wipe dirt off my hands. She's sitting on her knees, hands on hips, shaking her head.

"You know," I say. "If we stop by Enjoy the Silence, maybe one of your roommates would be home later by the time we're done."

She snaps her fingers. "Denise said she might be going. I can't believe I forgot."

It takes forever to get over there. I've only lived here a year, so I just drive where Melanie says, turning slowly so the wine doesn't bounce me around too bad. We seem to be close, there's a pizza-and-chicken joint with picnic tables out in the front, and blocks of trailers.

Melanie can't remember the address. We drive block after block, right turns, lefts... were we on this street already? I don't like the looks of this one, there's that same video store again, this one's pretty spooky, watch the glass. Then we turn a corner, and like a mirage, it's suddenly in front of us: a huge brick warehouse the size of a city block, with colored lights flashing from the top floor and the roof. Cars everywhere, just left there in the middle of the street, humming. Silent people are walking in, students by the look of them, plus one guy in one of those striped three-foot *Cat in the Hat* hats, which nobody seems to be looking at. Everyone's heads are down, fiddling with their Walkmans, but upstairs the shadows are bouncing around the huge windows, with not a sound from the building. We can hear sparrows, crickets, telephone wires on a utility pole creaking above us in the breeze.

She says, "Wonder what it sounds like in headphones."

"What's the frequency?" I say, and add, "Kenneth?" And we both laugh.

"Try 88.3," she says. "That's usually it."

We turn the radio on, hit scan. Scan can't find it, so I tap the button until we get there. Even sitting out here, where we couldn't be more than a hundred yards from the Enjoy the Silence transmitter, the techno beats are dampened by static. It sounds like a transmission from 1950s' Wyoming.

I turn off the engine, and the radio a minute after that, and we watch the shadows and colored lights grooving around upstairs. Four boys are perched like gargoyles up on the roof, bouncing their feet off the wall, bobbing their heads, staring at the Peachtree Plaza and into the night. Passing a huge bottle of water around.

"Looks cool," I say.

"Yeah," she says, her face up in the windshield. "Spooky." She unclips her seatbelt, and I feel the tiniest disappointment until I understand we're not going to get out of the car.

Ten minutes, and I'm buzzing and frantic, my hands rubbing her bare breasts harder than they should be.

"Oh," she says, but she's smiling. And then,"Aaron, you're shivering!" She's caught me: what women do, what they make me do.

"I'm not," I tell her. "I mean, I'm not! I'm not."

"Aaron," she says, and sits back. "You're going to hate me."

"What?"

"No, it's just, I don't really feel like going into this thing after all."

And before I can think of what I'm saying, I'm like, "The rave-thing? Let's go hang out at my place."

"Well, but, wait. What about your brother?" she says. "Like if he's been in touch, don't you want to see him?"

I don't say anything.

"Maybe he's tried you," she says, and then I remember the ringing phone, just as I was locking the door. My stomach tightens.

"Melanie, I can't look for him," I say. "Let's go find your keys. We haven't even checked to see if your roommates are in there."

She frowns. "I don't want to bother," she says. "We're on a date."

"I just—what if he's broken into my place, or he's hiding in the bushes with a knife or whatever?"

"Hiding with a knife?" she says. She runs her hand through my hair. There's a trace of a smile on her face.

"Or whatever."

"Oh... you mean, like, maybe your brother's been waiting all night for you to come home so he can jump out and attack you and kill you? Dude, I'm from Texas, and people do crazy shit there, and that's just..."

We both laugh. I lean forward and kiss her, nice and deep. We pull apart.

"He's probably waiting for you, right now," she says. "With a big, serrated, ten-inch blade..."

"Cut it out."

She sits back in her seat. "Sorry."

We're quiet for a minute. A tap on my window, and we both turn around to see two girls with headphones on, dancing outside the car, waving at us. There's not a sound. They blow us silent kisses and bounce away, their arms around each other's waists.

Melanie has to get me back to the Highlands from here, I'm completely clueless. But the wine's worn off so I can drive faster. We speed down the empty avenues, past downtown, and before I know it, before I want to be done with the drive, we're already looking for a parking spot.

We walk with her hand in my back pocket, and I unlock the gate under a low arch. The gate screeches softly, and I hold it open with my back so we can follow the concrete walkway into the courtyard between two rows of rumpled hedges.

Melanie pretends to peek beneath the hedges, behind them. "Caleb," she whispers. "Yo! Caleb!"

I shush her.

We're halfway down the walkway to my apartment door when we stop. There he is. Caleb's lying in front of my door. His face is turned toward us, eyes shut, hands flat on the concrete. I recognize the T-shirt now, from a trip I took to Vancouver: it says "Produit du Canada" and has a flag with a pot leaf where the maple leaf would go. Caleb's asleep on his olive duffel, his ski cap pressed under his face as a pillow. His mouth open. Put X's on his eyes, and he could be a cartoon drunk.

Melanie looks at me, then back down at my brother. And that's the first time I look at his face. He's been battered senseless: green-purple skin with raccoon bruises, one for each eye, and I don't recognize his nose.

"What the fuck."

"Oh my God," she says. "Aaron, he's really hurt, isn't he?" We walk, step by step, until we're close enough to squat, and I can reach to rub his shoulder.

When he doesn't wake up, Melanie reaches for his hair. She jerks her hand away, and I can see there's dried blood on his scalp.

She sits, cross-legged, and reaches over. "Caleb," she says.

The bruised eyes flutter and he licks his swollen upper lip. His eyes volley from mine to hers. "Hey, man," he says, and shuts his eyes to swallow.

Melanie says, "Aaron, where's your keys?"

While we wait outside, his eyelids flicker. He gasps and says, "I didn't do anything, Aaron."

"What's up with your face?" I say. "Was it that dude you were hanging out with tonight?"

"Aw, damn, man," he says. "That guy was gonna get me some weed I was gonna bring you, but we got jumped. I'm so tired." He smiles. "Hey, did Mom call you?"

I'm standing over him now, watching him, with my hands stuffed into my pockets. "We'll call her tomorrow," I say. "She really wants to talk."

And then Melanie's back, with a little ice pack from my freezer I've used only once, for a Bulldogs tailgate. "Caleb," she says, "can you stand up?"

"Oh, sure," he says, and pushes himself right off the ground. Suddenly, he's towering above us.

"Caleb, I want you to put this on your nose," she says, and hands him the pack. He nods and takes it and holds it up, pliant as a sick dog.

I scoop up his No Fear cap and drag his olive Nike bag into the apartment. She's already led him to the bed in the alcove, the bed I made this afternoon with clean sheets, military-tight, and fat white candles I've put up on the milk crates next to it, ready for action. There's only one lamp turned on in the apartment, right over the bed, and I stand back and watch in the gloom as Melanie unpeels the sheets and waits for Caleb to get in. He unlaces his huge boots, one by one, and they clump to the floor as he unwrenches them. He sits down on the bed and then folds up his knees to climb in. I groan a little, watching her fold my fresh blanket back up over him.

"Caleb, I want you to try to sleep with this ice on," she says. "Can you do that?"

There's the barest nod, and he puts the icepack back. He winces and sighs.

"I work with a doctor—I'll call him as soon as it's light out," she says, but he's closed his eyes. She watches him for a minute, then looks at me with her eyebrows creased.

I scoop all the magazines and TV remotes off the top of my Dad's army trunk, and once I've opened it, I find a blanket at the bottom that's not so scratchy.

When I look up, Caleb's got Melanie by the arm, and he's yanking her down to his face.

"Ow! Jesus!" she says, bracing herself against the bed. She makes a surprised peep as he palms the back of her head and pulls. She shoves his chest. I've forgotten to drop the blanket by the time I've reached them. I tug on her shoulder, cursing.

Then Caleb lets her go, and we both stumble backwards, and suddenly we're standing there, blinking. Caleb rolls over in the bed, turns his face from ours.

Melanie's flushed, her mouth creased. She looks away from me and rushes for the front door.

"Melanie, don't," I say. "Oh my God, I'm sorry I'm sorry please just—"

We scramble through the door and wind up sitting on the cement stoop. I pull the door shut, locking us out. Arms, knees, hands, everything trembles. I wrap the blanket around her and squeeze it tight.

"Melanie," I say. Please be okay, please be okay.

And I don't know what she sees on my face, but her shoulders soften, and she opens a flap of the blanket and I fit it around my shoulders, and we sit tight, we hug for two minutes, three, five, on my stoop, and then we lean back against the door.

Not a sound from inside, from Caleb. He's asleep, or passed out, with the lamp on. Will he let us in before dawn? Will he remember this? Melanie folds herself against me like a yardstick, holding me around my chest under the blanket. I close my eyes with my heart racing, and we sit wrapped up on the stoop, and I listen to us slowing down, breathing in and out.

## Automatic

### Rick Moody

I knew Barb from when I started going to AA meetings in my twenties. She played bass. She had that scar. Has it still. It went jaggedly down from her ear and then it took a right angle and headed for the edge of her mouth. She walked through a glass door when she was a kid. Barb was beautiful, in spite of this scar. But she didn't think so.

People like her didn't have that much to do with people like me. Barb didn't notice me till later. By then I had a girlfriend, also called Barb. This AA meeting we went to, it was exactly like a high school dance. Everyone was in their twenties or thirties, and there were all these guitar players around. All I wanted was to be able to talk to one of those beautiful women. Later, I did talk to some of them, and then I quit going there because an AA meeting should be about drinking, not about leather pants. One night I saw these two women, Barb and her friend Stacey, standing in the middle of the room. The meeting was emptying. They were mean looking, but they were radiant. Stacey looked Arabic, with dark hair that was dyed some kind of henna. She was longer and thinner than Barb was. Back then Barb was a tiny bit round with shoulder-length, dirty-blond hair. Stacey had a reputation as a poet, and she was trying to get a band together to play behind her when she did her performance poetry thing. She had ambitions for the project, like she would get such-and-such a famous producer to make the record, and then she would keep an eye on the charts.

I was piling up rejection letters for a screenplay.

There was no reason why, in the center of the room, with everyone leaving, these two women should be talking about me, but somehow I felt like they were talking about me. Maybe I wasn't quite as awkward as I always thought. This is what happens when you hang around AA meetings long enough. You improve.

People said Stacey was fickle, that I should avoid her. I asked her if I could go on a date with her anyhow. It was excruciating. Both the asking part and the date. When I wanted to seem presentable, I was dull. We ate in a café in the East Village, and she kept going out to smoke. She stood me up for date number two. Then she went through a bunch of guys, including the famous singer of some famous band. Meanwhile, Barb started seeing an alcoholic guitar player from Long Island. He didn't like hearing about her getting together with me very often. Maybe because I had a girlfriend also named Barb. That's much later. The people in this story aren't just in this story. Barb had this real boyfriend who knocked her up. Then they parted.

There was a civilian guy, non-alcoholic. He was my comrade. Anton. Kind of a strange-looking guy. Lanky like an antique coat rack, with a ghostly, terrified expression. Anton was the funniest person I ever knew. Also the most troubled. He was funny one day a month and that was a great day. No one could touch him. The rest of the month he was haunted by something or other. It varied. To say he was obsessive, that just gets at the most superficial part of it. He had bouts of indecision that lasted for months. Should he go to graduate school? Should he break up with this particular lover? What kind of bike should he buy?

Women liked Anton. When he turned his haunted expression on a woman, she felt a special validation. Anton really wanted their opinion. He really listened. Sometimes he listened to more than one woman at a time. There was always some woman who took up with him on the promise of one day a month. And then she hung in there during the dark weeks.

Barb had a lot of money. A whole lot more than I'll ever have. She was careless with it, I thought then, but maybe she wasn't careless at all. Maybe there was so much of it that she hadn't even made a dent in it, spending it on whatever. On the night all of us went to Coney Island, we were riding in Barb's Range Rover. A black Range Rover. I had never even owned a car, that's about how well I was doing on a freelance editor's wages.

I don't know what we ate. I don't know if we had dinner at all. You figure there had to be some scintillating dinner conversation. Why don't I ever remember bon mots? Since then I've met lots of interesting people. I heard a famous news anchor tell off-color jokes at a cocktail party once. He said he'd told these jokes to Ehud Barak, too. I can't remember any of them. And I can't remember any of the stuff that Barb or Stacey or Anton said.

But I remember the interior of the black Range Rover, the smell of leather in a new Range Rover. And I remember that Barb had this early work of electronica, that idiom of popular music which featured many synthesizers. An idiom which seems to have come and gone. Maybe it was the novelty of big beat, the simplicity of the roar of big beat, in the back of the Range Rover at night. We'd hit some open traffic pattern that was inconceivable. We were going through Brooklyn fast, not around the perimeter. The digital effects on the record began to cycle through and around the car. The drum samples were from soul records from the '60s and '70s, and the whole thing was bouncing around the interiors of the Range Rover. Everyone was slouching. The boys, Anton and me, we were hunched down in the back, hunched down just like we were teenagers, and the girls were up front, and there was no conversation, because in order to say anything, you had to yell.

Every now and then Anton would shout something really funny though. He was definitely on. It was his one night a month, and his timing was good, and the delivery was so offhanded and self-effacing that it was half stand-up and half Samuel Beckett or

Harold Pinter. It was night in Brooklyn, and the streets were mostly empty, and we were driving. What could be better? We were breakbeat junkies.

How many car rides like that had we had? We all had a lot of these car rides. I remember driving with my stepbrother back from somewhere out in Jersey, in his Jeep, one of those two-seaters that bounces around a lot. A potential rollover accident. My stepbrother was playing Rush in his Jeep. This was incredibly embarrassing. And yet almost all loud music, when designed to interrupt the flow of polite but unnecessary conversation, was a blessing. I'd heard entire Grateful Dead concerts when young, driving around with my sister and brother. I remember playing *Dub Housing* by Pere Ubu in a car on the way to my high school reunion and pissing off the other people in the car so badly that I'm not sure they have spoken to me since.

Libido was our theme. Desire swirled in the Range Rover, winding itself around the music. Everybody was temporarily available. Or almost temporarily available. Everybody was into everybody. Or everyone was into the way a group can recycle energy, like it's a nuclear reaction. We weren't trying to impress the neighborhood with our musical choices, the way local guys tried to do with their hip hop. Maybe they just didn't have air conditioning. Barb had air conditioning. We were a complete circuit. Some kind of joy was making its way around the car. It was a complete thing, undiminished by the length of the trip out to Coney Island. We ditched the car under an overpass. I couldn't believe Barb was going to park her new Range Rover in an unsecured location. She seemed not to worry about stuff like this.

Stacey had a ritual involving Skee Ball. She lived the carny life. She knew people at the side show. The guy who punched nails into his nose. But we never got to the side show. No, there was a point to the adventure, and the point was the Cyclone. The way the tracks shuddered in the wood frame. The screams. The screams were nothing, at first, from a distance. They were amusement park screams. But when you got close and you heard the cars tip over the first lip, the first steep drop that is the Cyclone's great accomplishment, those screams were good. You could feel them down in your bloodstream. Rollercoasters get their power from the possibility of mortality. If you couldn't die on them, there wouldn't be anything scary about it. Wouldn't be anything thrilling.

The night was good. The stars were good. You could actually see them. The boardwalk life of Coney Island was good. All those photos of Coney Islands of the past, remember? Bodies packed in, on the beach? America's playground. There was a hustling aspect to Coney Island. The guys running the rides looked like junkies. They seemed like they had not been amused in years. People were going to get mugged.

We divided up into pairs. I was with Stacey, even though she'd stood me up that time. She and I were in the front car. Barb and Anton were back a ways. I was really happy about the part of the ride where Stacey's body was going to jam against my body. On the first big turn. I didn't have to do anything to make sure her body jammed against mine, it would just happen. That meant that there was no quarrel with the fact. Automatic events were meant to be, and there were no worries about them. Certain sounds, like screams, these were manifestations of the order of things, automatic events, and being on the lip of that big 8% downgrade, or whatever it was, this was a manifestation of the order of things. Being in a car on the Cyclone, when I was young, this was a manifestation of the order of things, this was automatic, and Barb's scar, juxtaposed with her really beautiful smile, this was a manifestation of the order of things, this was automatic, and Anton's brilliance, this was a manifestation of the order of things, and here we were, poised at the top of the Cyclone, before heading down, and all was right, and it seemed like Stacey was being lifted off of the bench, and I could hear her screaming, and I could hear screaming behind me, a pair of teenagers in love, a girl with a pile of blond hair, they were screaming, and then way back in the car, I could hear something resembling a scream come from Barb, though Anton was probably not the type to get too worked up, because he preferred some kind of affectionate ridicule of the whole matter later on. I was next to Stacey and now we were going around the curve, and she was flattening me against the side of the car, that grimy car where fifty thousand kids had shrieked this summer, never mind the forty years of teenagers, the teenagers in love, doo wop teenagers, beatniks, hippies, Hispanic kids, African-American kids, Russian kids, Polish kids, Jewish kids, Islamic kids. Everyone rode the Cyclone, through all of modern history, because it was automatic, and they should have been coming around the last turn with a wild girl, a poet, and they should have been paying the despairing rollercoaster operators, to permit a second trip. Stacey and I were in the front again and we were going around again, and we were at the top again, and again we were on our way down—

Not many nights as good as that night.

Things have gone wrong since then. Business hasn't turned out like I thought it was going to. I have had instants of certainty that suffering will be the next knock at my door. Still, there was a moment when the chain was dragging us up the first incline and all I wanted to do was wrap my arms around Stacey. This was just a feeling. This was automatic. She had lips that were almost impossible not to kiss. I guess I felt the same way about Barb. What could have been easier? Anton was my best friend, just my best friend. Poised there, with the moonlight on the sea before us, that high up, we were part of something. I don't know what. Maybe the end of youth. Later, Stacey and I did kiss, after a game of Scrabble in the East Village. I kissed her in the hall. She was a great kisser. And Barb had her kid. Anton and I had a falling out over something I said, or maybe something he said. Stacey bought a grand piano. Wrote a detective novel. Anton got famous in his way. They were prone to bad habits, they were my friends, and they were perfect, more or less.

The night is not a symbol. And youth is not a symbol. Avoid making kisses a symbol. Avoid making music a symbol. Avoid making symbols of inclines and declines. Avoid making the Cyclone a symbol, you know? It's perfect as an idea. It's automatic as a memory.

## Stalker's Paradise

**Richard Rushfield**

I can still remember a time when my front life seemed the greatest of all possible worlds. Young single woman at loose in the big, exciting city; dinner parties, shows, music, constantly asked out on dates by a line of cute, semi-eligible guys. And on the holidays, I went home to see my family.

And this was plenty, really it was. I loved the city. I liked my job. And although I always seemed to unearth some fatal immaturity in the guys I dated, they were knights in shining cargo pants compared to the creeps back home. From your daytimer's perspective, I'm sure you assume I was abject and desperate, but that's not how it was. I was really just fine.

But now, that life looks like a torture chamber equipped with instruments invented specially to burrow into the most sensitive crannies of my soul. Everyday at work I cringe in agony, counting the seconds until I am free. People try to make plans with me and I tell them I'm going out of town for the weekend. I turn down dates. I haven't seen my family in a year. Because the truth of this city, if you really want to know, is that all the work and sex and dinner parties are not what makes this place hum. When the night falls, the city is a stalker's paradise. And that's when the real Amy comes alive.

The guy who drove me into The Community was the last person you'd picture driving a girl insane. At first glance, that is. But when you know more about stalkers you find out that, in fact, he's a fairly typical inciter. Marcus is his name. You see people like him on the street every day and never notice; quiet, middle-management or middle-something types, the most miss-worthy guys in the world. He has this habit when he gets uncomfortable of chewing on the corner of his sleeve that makes people want to kick his teeth in. You'd never guess that someone like him could push someone as together as I was off my rocker. But guys like him do, every day of the year.

Marcus and I started going out not long after I broke up with Teddy, the flashy bassist who I'd stuck it out with for a year. I was twenty-six, still recovering and definitely not looking for anything serious when I met Marcus. Seated next to each other at Tanya and Gary's wedding, Marcus stood out only as quiet and non-threatening. The non-chemistry between us was instantly clear. I recall during the best man's toast glancing over at him and seeing him looking at me, smiling nervously, and thinking, "No way." But during dinner we chatted fine, I guess, spark-free but it wasn't painful. So when he asked me out, all I thought was, you've got to get back on the horse sometime. One dinner, what's the harm?

Our first date was indeed harmless. He took me to dinner and then we strolled by the park. Everything about the night was nice, in a "yeah, I guess it was nice" way. The Shrimp Shack where he took me was fine, not totally inappropriate but not even slightly exciting either, a place just this side of I'd-be-a-bitch-to-complain-about-it. We chatted about where we were from, how many brothers we have and found just enough in common so that conversation wasn't a total bridge collapse. Strolling, he extended his arm for me and I placidly took it. He sorted of patted my hand and squeezed it with his arms against his torso, but didn't try for anything more. When he dropped me off, he sensed the mood correctly and kissed me on the cheek. So when he called the next day and asked for another date, I said, why not? It could be far worse and come to think of it, lately it has been. So I rode along, sinking deeper into the abyss of no connection, my sense that it was better than staying home alone fading by the hour.

It wasn't until our fourth date that everything changed. We made an encore visit to the Shrimp Shack. ("You liked it there, didn't you?" he asked in the car.) We ordered and sat in silence, glancing awkwardly at each other. He nibbled on his sleeve and I noticed the mustard stain on the front of his shirt. I remembered him dropping a hot dog on himself the last time we went out. I waited for him to speak, to start conversation, but he just smiled like he didn't even notice the awkwardness. It's now, or never, I thought, and took a deep breath.

"Listen, Marcus," I began.

"Can I borrow your phone?"

"What?"

"Your phone. I need to make a quick call."

"Ummm... sure." I was so thrown off-balance that I just obediently fished into my purse and handed over the phone.

"Thanks." He nodded and walked out the front door.

It's hard to gauge how long I actually sat alone. Although it felt like nineteen hours, it couldn't really have been. Judging by the family at the next table, who had time to order and eat before Marcus returned, I'd clock his absence at about 35 minutes. More important, though, was how I changed while he was gone. My weary determination to call things off evolved into something much bigger: a parasite burrowed into my heart and took root. By the time Marcus came back, outrage, confusion, and a burning pain to know whom he was talking to had driven me to tear my napkin into a million tiny pieces.

Marcus handed back my phone with a quick "Thanks" and started blabbing about some work project without so much as a nod of the head at his rudeness. My swordfish plate had arrived while he'd been out and I picked at it, unable to swallow the now cold and mushy filet. Marcus, however, tore into his mahi with total abandon, unbelievably oblivious to its ruined state. Talking with his mouth full, he was more animated than I'd ever seen him. I fumed, 'Doesn't this jerk know he's about to get dumped?' but he rattled on right through dinner until he finally announced, "You don't mind if I drop you off right after this? I've gotta go do something. Hey, what happened to your napkin?"

After that night, my break-up plans melted in the caldron of my bubbling frustration. As Marcus was alternately hideously boring and spirit-wrenchingly irritating, he wormed under my skin and left me scratching at myself like a lunatic, unable to touch the source of my pain. One night out he'd be a total wet noodle, and I'd breathe a sigh of satisfaction, thinking, 'You see, you were all worked up about nothing. This guy is eminently dumpable.' But then he'd make a date with me and cancel at the last minute just saying, "There's stuff I gotta do." Another time, when we planned to go to the movies, he took me for a coffee at Starbucks and drove me straight home.

I'd burn to ask him, "Is there someone else?" But that would imply there was a me, which was still the last idea I wanted to give him. So instead, when he left the room I'd look through his appointment book. It was filled with cryptic notes like "CKR to DW2 for re-down43." I looked at the box for that night, where our date should've been. The box was blank.

I explained to my friend Nora what was going on.

"That guy? Amy, he is so not your type. Not anywhere close to your league."

"I know," I nodded. "That's what makes it so annoying."

"Ewwww," she said. "Tell him to buzz off."

"I can't yet. For some reason, I just need to work through this."

Nora glanced at me sideways, a look of confusion and pity that made me hate myself for confiding in her.

And so I came to stalking. It was our two-month anniversary and I'd bought tickets to the opera which I actually hate, but wanted to make the night special. I'd had my hair done and wore the salmon dress I'd been saving for a special occasion. I planned to break up right after the show.

I don't know why I hadn't seen it coming but when I hung up the phone, after assuring him that it was okay, we could go out next week, I felt like I'd been blindsided by a quadruple load U-Haul maxi. I paced the floors, fuming in my salmon dress, and decided that I could not sit still for this.

Marcus lived on the second floor of a little brownstone walk-up. I positioned myself on the sidewalk out front, hopping up and down to catch a peek inside, but I could only see the ceiling. I crossed the little street and craned my neck to try and see better. A white-bearded man, standing with a little dog and smoking a pipe, looked at me curiously and I shot a poison-tipped glare back. The lights in Marcus's front room were out but I saw his shadow float across his back wall. Frustration blazed; I had to practically tie myself up to keep from pressing his buzzer.

I crossed back over the street and checked that no one was looking. The old man was joined by a younger one and they both stared at me, but I was past caring.

"Don't you have anything better to do?" I hissed. I heard them chuckle as I climbed up onto a garbage can and balanced on tiptoes, finally gaining a glimpse inside. It looked empty. No lights, no shadows, no movement.

"Amy?" I heard suddenly and my heart dove into my ankles. Marcus had come out the front door and stood by the garbage can wearing a bemused smirk that made me want to kick his face in. He wore his black mock-turtleneck and leather coat, dressed for a night out. "What are you doing up there?"

I climbed down, stumbling as I landed and faced him. "Where the hell are you going?" I jabbed a finger into his face.

"I told you, something came up."

"What came up?"

He smirked more and actually patted me on the head. "Oh, Amy," he said. "I didn't know you had such strong feelings. Why didn't you speak up?"

Steam billowed from my ears. "I don't have strong feelings! I mean, they're strong but not like you think they are. Just — where are you going?"

While I sputtered, Marcus flagged down a cab. "I'll make it up to you. I promise. Next weekend."

"Next weekend!" I howled as the cab zoomed away. I stood in the street gaping and was nearly run down by a moped. "Arrgh!" I screamed as I tumbled to the pavement, ripping my salmon dress. I sat on the ground, trembling with rage, cursing myself and him in equal servings.

Suddenly a hand, a soft but powerful, decaying old man's hand emerging from the sleeve of a tweed jacket, reached out for mine.

"There's a better way, you know."

I looked up, the old man with the pipe gazed down. Something in his sad, knowing eyes instantly calmed me. I don't know why but right then I felt like he understood what had happened and that it would be okay. I took his hand and was pulled to my feet.

"What do you mean, a better way?"

His white beard curved into a grin, eyes twinkling. "You've never done this before, have you?"

"Done what?" I noticed behind his back the younger man stood watching with a serious, concerned look on his face.

"Followed someone. Someone you love."

"No. Of course not. Why should I?" The old and young man both chuckled.

"That's right. Why should you? Why indeed?" They guffawed to each other. I waited for them to explain the joke and noticed it was getting cold.

"What's your name, young lady?" the old man asked.

I told him.

"I am Benjamin Leopold," he bowed, sweeping off his cap with an elaborate flourish. "But I'm known to my friends as Leo."

"Hi, Leo."

"And my young friend here: this is Roosevelt." The younger man waved at me but didn't speak. "Now, tell me, Amy. Would you like to find where your friend has gone?"

I didn't know what to say, so I just nodded.

"We can take care of this," he stated matter-of-factly.

"How? I haven't even told you his name."

Again, Leo and Roosevelt chuckled at each other, rolling their eyes at some inside joke. "Come back here this time tomorrow and we'll have all the information you desire."

"Wow, ummm… thanks?" I was creeped out and comforted at the same time.

"But before you go, Amy, I can only help you on one condition: Do you love him?"

I thought for a moment. Feelings churned that were impossible to describe. I recognized elements of hate, of anger, of sadness, of hurt, of obsession. But all together, I didn't know what they added up to. It was a blend I'd never experienced before but it was stronger than any emotion I'd ever known. For a moment, I savored the ferocity of it, the sharp edge. I suppose this is love, I thought. What else could it be? I saw myself kissing Marcus, then hurting him badly.

"Yes," I answered softly. "Yes, I do."

"Good," Leo nodded. "We'll see you here. Same time tomorrow."

The next day, I grabbed the phone a thousand times but somehow fought back the urge to call Marcus. That night his little street was empty and quiet. I shivered, feeling ridiculous. Marcus's lights were on.

"Boo," a smoky voice said. Leo appeared. Down the block, the younger one shuffled towards us.

I followed Leo down a few steps below someone's porch and stood in the surprisingly warm grotto underneath. The Dugout, as they called it, was furnished with a sofa and easy chair.

Incredible, I thought, that so vast a space could squeeze under those steps and be invisible from the street.

"You spend a lot of time here?" I asked.

I saw a trace of sadness moisten Leo's kindly eyes. "This is where Roosevelt and I stand watch." I glanced around. All the questions that came to mind seemed rude to ask, so I just nodded.

"It's very comfortable here, really," said Roosevelt.

"Now, this man of yours, this... Marcus, I believe," Leo drawled.

"How did you get out his name?" I asked.

"You recall the moped that almost ran you over, the one following the taxi? That was a friend of ours. She was... well," he chuckled. "Keeping an eye on the man driving the taxi."

"That's quite a coincidence."

"Not at all. Not at all. Our friends are everywhere. At the restaurant where they ate, for instance, another of our friends was at the bar, taking notes on another table. We got word out in time and he was able to notice that your Marcus ate with a group of four people. Business associates of his, it turns out."

"Just a business dinner?" I asked.

"Well, almost. Apparently, there was one woman there. Late 20s, blonde hair, about 5'6". Marcus seemed to have his arm around her back for much of the night. But it's not clear whether she noticed."

"I see." That was Sarah; I knew it. Marcus had introduced her to me at a party and I'd been grossed out when I caught him leering as she walked away. I felt completely exposed in front of

Leo & Roosevelt, but saw their eyes filled with nothing but sympathy, and started crying.

"I'm very sorry." Leo patted me on the back.

"It doesn't necessarily mean there's anything going on," Roosevelt said.

"What happened after dinner?" I choked out.

"Marcus took her home in a taxi but he did not go in."

"Did he kiss her goodnight?"

"We don't know for certain. I'm sorry."

I nodded and tried to pull myself together. "What is this network?"

Leo lit his pipe. "In this great city, a million things are possible. By day, strolling in the park you see lovers hand in hand. Love blooms. Everyone is happy. But that's not always the story. Hiding in the shadows are a million loves gone wrong. Thwarted but not dead, we are the loves that live on after their sun has set."

"So what do you do?"

"We keep an eye on the people we love."

"You stalk them?"

Leo winked and smiled. "Yes. Yes, we do."

We were silent. A car drove past, sending a gentle gust of chilly wind down the stairs.

Roosevelt said quietly, "We look after them."

Leo pointed at the building above us. "My ex-wife lives here. We've been divorced for over thirty years. She's twice remarried. But I swore to love her forever and I'm not giving up."

I felt repulsed, but also tremendously sympathetic. I wanted to hug them both. I thought of Marcus and what a wreck I'd become.

"It's very hard... very hard to love... sometimes," my words gasped out between sobs. "I don't know how to do this." I covered my face with my lambskin gloves.

I felt Leo's arms wrap around me. "It's okay. You don't have to be alone any more. From now on, we'll help you keep this young fellow close by."

We climbed back up to the street. It was almost midnight. Leo glanced up.

"She's in for the night."

Roosevelt nodded, "Miriam's at the movies with her college friends."

"Will you want to wait?" Leo asked.

"Naw, they'll just sit up talking all night. And last time Karin came over, she pepper-sprayed me."

I followed the pair down the block.

They nodded to people we passed, a man sitting in an ice cream truck window, an old woman tying her shoelaces on a stoop, people walking a few yards behind other people who nodded back and whispered, "Hi, Leo."

We turned down an alley. At the dead end, Leo leaned against a trash dumpster. "This is getting heavier," he moaned as they pushed it aside to reveal a doorway. Leo took out an old-fashioned brass key and we stepped through.

Inside, a cavernous warehouse-sized room bustled with hundreds of people shuffling business-like through the thick, smoky air. Along one huge wall, a man on a ladder scribbled entries on a giant chalkboard, which seemed to track movements of stalkees. A loudspeaker called out, "All operatives on the West 1500s: be on the lookout tonight for a black Honda Civic—license plate U362DEW—bearing 15336 and female unknown."

At a mahogany-paneled bar, we ordered some hot spiked ciders and took them to a corner booth. Everyone nodded to Leo respectfully.

"He's like the mayor," Roosevelt whispered.

Sitting in the corner booth, Leo held court. A stream of stalkers paid their respects and asked for advice.

"Restraining order?" Leo laughed to one. "If we let restraining orders slow us down then the whole world could just run around behind our backs and we wouldn't have a clue."

The next night, I raced from work to Marcus's street, arriving just after dark. Leo and Roosevelt were already at their posts. "We registered Marcus's name at the club, so from now on the whole Community will be on the lookout."

I could see from the lights that Marcus was inside his apartment. Leo had me draw a layout of the three rooms. Over the next few nights, he taught me how to judge from the shadows exactly where Marcus was inside. Studying the reflections closely, we were even able to make out the tiny red glow from the answering machine, blinking if he had a message, faster if he had a few.

For the first week, to my surprise, Marcus stayed home and no one visited him. He just spent a lot of time on the phone and a lot of time watching TV. Leo taught me how to tail him when he went out, but I was a klutz about it and nearly got spotted while following him on his errands.

Through The Community, I found out that Sarah was out of town for the week. That's why he was staying in, I figured. The next day, Marcus called me at work.

"What're you doing tonight?" he asked.

"Ummm... not much? Why?"

"I thought you might want to go out." My heart raced with excitement. I was going to get him and sort this out before things got really weird. But in the same breath I felt sort of uncomfortable, like I was breaking a boundary by talking to him, making plans.

"Sure," I said, not at all sure. "That would be great."

"Okay, I'll pick you up at — Oh, damn, wait a minute," he swore. "I gotta go to that thing tonight."

"That thing?"

"Just that thing I promised someone I'd do. But next week for sure. Gimme a call, 'kay?"

Before I could answer, he hung up.

Over lunch, Nora tried to make plans with me but I brushed her off and after work raced across town to Marcus's street. I arrived just in time to see him pulling away in a taxi. From around the corner, Roosevelt walked up. I grabbed him.

"That cab! Did you get the number?"

"No, Amy, I'm sorry."

I swore and shook his thin frame. "Damn it, what good are you people?" And then I sat down on the curb and fought back a crying fit that threatened to break loose.

Roosevelt gingerly patted my shoulder. "It's okay. Sometimes they get away. It happens."

"But he's going to meet her tonight. I know it."

"And you'll be here waiting. They can't get away from that." I looked up at Roosevelt, his timid gray eyes filling with concern, and hugged him. His fragile ribcage crackled against mine.

"How long did you and Miriam go out for?" I asked.

"Oh, Miriam and I never went out. I hardly knew her before this."

"Really?"

"She was the most beautiful girl in my school. She would've never gone out with me."

"But then how did you get started?"

"Well..." He sat down next to me, continued on, his big earnest eyes completely free of guile or deceit. "I guess back when we were kids I used to stalk her a bit. Nothing serious, I'd just kind of ride my bike past her house a lot. In my mind I'd make believe she was my girlfriend and I swore I'd always love her. It's kind of what gave my life meaning during those awful years. Then we went to college and I didn't see her for a whole decade until one day, after I moved to the city and I was feeling lost, I ran into her on the streets and everything just clicked."

I touched his arm. "Don't you ever think about moving on? Having a real girlfriend?"

He looked down. "Sometimes. Yes, I guess I do. But this is a good life. Leo's been very good to me, like no one before. These people are all so nice. And I get to see Miriam every day. I really do love her. I know that now." I hugged Roosevelt again and told him I'd help watch until Marcus came home.

A beautiful woman slinked through the door, dramatically removed her coat and walked over to our table. When she spotted me there, she looked me up and down and turned for the bar. She was tall with severe brown hair cut at an angle across her perfect nose and mouth, which looked like they had been set in ivory. Or ice.

"Is she okay?" I asked.

"Yolanda? She's fine... fine," Leo drawled. "Just a little territorial. Give her time, she'll get used to you."

"Why are there so few women stalkers?" I asked.

Leo chuckled as though I'd said something funny. "Well, that is the question, isn't it? It's like asking why there are so few women cable installers? Why, indeed?"

"Maybe women don't need to stalk," Roosevelt said so softly I could hardly hear, nervously glancing at me. "Maybe things just work out for them."

"I dunno. All my women friends are messes... None of them have anything to lose by stalking."

"You wanna know why?" a woman's voice said sharply. Yolanda was back, holding a tall glass of dark iced liquid. She slid into the booth, glaring from under her bangs. "Because dames got no sense of honor."

I made a peep to protest but she talked me down.

"Oh, I know you love this guy. Right now you're all worked up about him and you say you're not going to let go no matter what. But you know what, Annie—"

"Amy."

"Annie. Amy. Annie. You know what? First better thing passes your way, you'll walk out on him and the whole life. First time you wake up with a tummy ache, you're going to stay in bed and watch the Oxygen network right through your shift while your man strolls out and takes your kid sister for a carriage ride through Central Park."

"I don't have—"

"I know you don't have a sister. That's just the point. You're not made for this and that's why these joes here, if they had any smarts left, wouldn't get too attached because next time the wind blows, you'll be out the door and down the street like the autumn leaves."

I glanced over at Leo and Roosevelt. They looked down, as though confirming what Yolanda said.

"That's not true. I love Marcus."

"What do you know about love? Do you love this guy enough to stay out here for fifteen years? That's how long I've been out here. Fifteen years this March. Think you'll make that?"

"Yes," I nodded. "I think so."

"Do you think you could cut off your ear and send it to your guy? You think you could love as much as Van Gogh?"

"I hope—I hope it won't come to that."

"Right," she spat. "I give you a week." And as she took a sip of her drink, she pulled back her hair, revealing an expanse of smooth ivory flesh where her right ear should've been.

I settled into the routine of life in The Community. A few people at my office were on the watch list, so the days I was supposed to be working I spent keeping tabs on them. Jonathan, who sat two desks over and whom I'd made out with at a party once, was being stalked. I'd strain to listen to his personal calls and turn the notes in at the club. On the way out, I'd grab the used message pad off the reception desk. The club staff sorted through the old messages for the names of our targets.

The reports I got on Marcus, however, were pretty inconclusive. Our people at his office were 95% sure that whoever he was seeing didn't work there. Sarah, the tramp I'd suspected, was now clearly involved with someone else. Apparently Marcus usually took his lunch at his desk and placed few personal calls, other than to me. We still talked a couple times a week; he'd make plans to get together which he'd break, each cancellation coming closer and closer to the actual time of the date, until I showed up at his door and found a note: 'Next week, for sure!' On these nights our trackers either lost him or reported him with a group. I asked Leo if it was strange that I was still in contact with my target.

"Oh no," he said. "Many keep up decent relations for years before things settle down."

More and more, I found myself estranged from the relationship culture that my peers reveled in. Every time I watched one of those young-urbanites-and-their-sex-problems TV shows that I used to be addicted to, I'd find myself sneering. "Pathetic," I'd guffaw. Real love, I now understood, was not about endlessly sampling in search of a 'connection' or 'chemistry.' It wasn't about 'communication' or 'understanding.' Real love was about picking someone and sticking to him. No matter what. Anything less was tourism.

I'd share these thoughts with Roosevelt each night in The Dugout. With him and Leo and the others, I found a society that valued devotion and commitment, where emotions were built to last. I asked Roosevelt about Miriam, "Don't you ever just want to kiss her until she suffocates to death?"

He nodded grimly. "Sometimes, when I think about how she's walked away from what we should've had, I have thoughts like that. But mostly, I just want to make her happy."

"Do you think it will stop?" I asked him, huddled close to block the wind blowing down the stairs.

"What do you mean?"

"I just wonder, Roosevelt. You've been out there so long, where does this lead to?"

He shook his head. "I can't think about that."

"But what if Miriam never changes her mind?"

"She's made her choice and I've made mine. I don't have any regrets."

Winter set in and the sleet began to pour down at regular, remorseless intervals, dripping down the stairs and sloshing up the Dugout floor. The golden autumn of stalking was over and I got some satisfaction in seeing that I was not among the many freshmen who broke from the frost and gave up their posts. As conditions grew rougher, every night at the club those determined ones still remaining drew tighter. I began to feel like a grizzled veteran, at home with the only people who understood.

Even Yolanda warmed to me a little: one night as I went back to my post she snarled, "Sweetie, that red scarf's gonna get you spotted a thousand miles away."

On those cold, wet nights, Roosevelt seemed like my only ally against a vicious, hostile world. Marcus's calls to me were tapering off and my calls to him were ignored completely. I was convinced there was someone else even though he seemed to spend his nights alone, often at his computer. I longed to see his phone bill but he never put it in his garbage, saving it, I knew, for his tax records. The only way to find out for sure would be to break in to his apartment and I wasn't ready to cross that line yet, although many advised me I should get over my lingering daytimer's scruples already.

Roosevelt had his problems, too. One night he appeared, out of breath, fighting back tears, oblivious to the cold rain slicing in hard sheets across his face. Miriam, he had learned, had gotten engaged to that lawyer. Roosevelt had been told this by a contact the previous night but hadn't believed it until, having followed her to dinner, he spotted her waving around a diamond ring on her fourth finger.

I pulled him out of the rain, got him out of his soaked blazer and hugged him tight. He leaned his head on my shoulder and cried for hours.

"Shhhh... this is good," I comforted him. "This is when you'll show her how you really feel. No, no. You won't give up."

We stayed all night, Roosevelt rocking back and forth in my arms, talking about our resolve, how our love for them went so much deeper than theirs could for anyone. As the chill set in I took off my gloves and tried to warm his hands, rubbing them back and forth between mine.

"We're going to be okay," I told him. I looked up. His eyes, the tears now stopped, caught and held mine. Blushing, I looked back down and saw our hands, the fingers intertwining.

"Your nose...," he said to me.

"Yes?"

"From this angle, it looks just like Miriam's."

"Ohhhh, Roosevelt," I cried. I grabbed his cold wet face and kissed him.

Whether Roosevelt and I would've been drawn together under normal circumstances is questionable. Our bond was so defined by our situation that as much as I tried to picture us dating in college or meeting at a cocktail party, I could never remove us from the little corner we had painted ourselves into.

After checking on the status of our marks, making sure they were tucked in for the night, seething at the comfort of their warm nests, and careful to check that Leo wasn't coming by, Roosevelt and I would collide in the Dugout, our bodies drawn together by frustration and rage desperate for an outlet. Afterwards, we'd lie together, the chilling air rudely nestling in pockets of sweat, and our thoughts would turn away from each other, to the people across the street.

"Maybe I should just peek out, check on Miriam."

"I guess so. Marcus might go out, too."

Roosevelt noticed my wounded look. "We can't forget what we're here for."

I bit my lip and shook my head and told him in complete earnestness, "I would never, never do that."

But it was getting harder to remember Marcus.

One day he called me at work. These calls had become so routine that the surprise of the fresh disappointments had almost lost their sting. I sleepwalked through our conversations, reciting my part but feeling numb rather than outraged.

"So what are you up to tonight?"

"Nothing," I mumbled.

"Want to come over?"

"Okay."

"What's wrong?"

"Nothing. I said, 'Okay.' "

"You sound like you don't really want to."

"I do. I want to come over." I dredged up an ounce of emotion to throw into my voice.

"Great, it's about time we hung out. Why don't you drop by at—" He paused, inhaling for dramatic effect.

"You have plans you forgot about?"

"Yeah, I just remembered. I'm so, so sorry."

"Plans with some people you can't really explain?"

"Yeah, well, um, kinda."

We were silent for a moment. I had come this far, my head was clear. I dove in.

"Marcus, you don't have any plans, do you?"

"What are you talking about? Of course I do."

"Uh-huh."

"Really, this person. I mean, yeah. I have lots."

"Okay, Marcus. Have fun."

I heard him yelling "Wait!" as I hung up.

I thought about my post and realized there was no reason to go tonight. Marcus would be sitting home alone, browsing a video store or at worst going to dinner with some work friends. What if this was the night he really did have a date? I wondered. But when I tried to picture it, suddenly I didn't care. I thought about going to see a movie for the first time in a year.

And then I thought about Roosevelt, sitting lonely in the Dugout, nursing the flickering candle of his love for Miriam. I wanted to tell him how it felt to be free of that and that he and I could turn these loves on each other. But I wondered too, whether I was taking advantage of him, whether I was worse than one of those empty-headed daytimers. Had I come into this world, faked a love just to become a parasite off the true loves of others?

At the club much later that night, Roosevelt and I sat in the center of a crowded booth, both deep in thoughts. I couldn't focus on the story Lars was telling about following his ex on vacation to Turkey because I was so immersed in thinking about how to get Roosevelt out of here so we could be alone. Amidst all the chatter I felt invisible until Andre pointed us out, "Hey! Look at those two. They've drifted off to outer space together."

Roosevelt and I blushed simultaneously.

"Is everything alright, kids?" Leo asked.

"Sure. Everything's fine," Roosevelt stammered.

Andre kept at it. "Don't you guys ever find spending so much time together distracting? I mean, if I was locked away with someone all night, every night, I know I'd get ideas sooner or later."

Roosevelt looked like he wanted to die. Under the table, I tapped my foot against his and felt him pull away.

Yolanda leaned close and smiled at me, her smile laced with daggers. "So how's Marcus, Amy?" she whispered.

We left the group and silently walked through the snowy streets back to the post.

I was the first to speak. "Is everything okay?"

Roosevelt nodded and smiled grimly. "Yeah, yeah. Fine. I was just thinking."

"What about?"

"Well, Miriam and that man are starting vacation tomorrow. Three weeks. I was just wondering how things are going to be when they're gone."

"You mean with us?"

He nodded.

"How do you think they'll be?"

"I don't know... it's just... I'm getting carried away. I don't want to lose everything I've built up."

At the opening of the Dugout, I rubbed Roosevelt's tense back as he watched Miriam and her fiancé load their luggage into a taxi and drive away.

"Sit down," I said.

"I need to keep watch for awhile."

"But they're gone."

"They might come back. They might have left the oven on... They might... Oh God!" Roosevelt collapsed onto the sofa, clasping his face in his hands, turning from me. "You don't understand anything about this!" he hissed.

"What do you mean? Of course I do. We're..." I thought for a moment, not believing myself, but said it anyway, "We're in the same boat."

"Oh sure," he snickered.

"What do you mean by that?"

"Since we've started this, you don't even care about Marcus anymore. I'll bet you don't even know where he is tonight. I've been covering for you with everyone, but it's true. You've given up on him. "

"It's not. Sure. He's probably watching TV, like he does every night."

"But you don't know. I know. I never lose track of Miriam. How can you pretend you understand love when Marcus could be out getting lap dances, for all you care?"

I never wanted to hold Roosevelt as bad as I did at that moment, to tell him I wanted a love as strong as his, that I envied him that and wanted to try to find that with him, rather than alongside him.

But before I could, something funny happened. I looked up into the door of the dugout and saw a figure standing there watching us. It was Marcus with a sheepish, embarrassed grin on his face, chewing on his sleeve.

"I'm sorry," he mumbled. "Am I interrupting?"

Roosevelt stopped sobbing and gazed upon Marcus with awe. "No. Absolutely not, sir. We were just talking."

Marcus nodded. "I was just wondering. I haven't seen you out on the street lately, and I wondered if everything was okay?"

I glared at him with contempt. "Sure, Marcus. It's just swell."

"Oh, good. Good." His face brightened a bit, a little of his pathetic swagger returned. "Well, then maybe you want to get some coffee?"

I looked at Roosevelt, who turned his back to me, offering me no refuge from this.

"I guess so," I shrugged finally. "Sure."

"Oh great. Let me just get my— oh you know what?"

"You've got plans?"

"Doesn't that suck? Well," he grinned, "gotta run. You guys keep up the good work here, okay?" He walked back up the steps and hailed a cab, driving away.

I looked to Roosevelt, my eyes pleading, and he stared at me coldly, like a wounded dog, until all of a sudden he shook it off.

"This is it. You can find out who she is. Did you get his cab number?"

"Um, no," I mumbled.

"That's okay. The cab was pointed uptown. I'll run to the club and put out an APB. This is great. Tonight, we'll track him down." Roosevelt hugged me, threw on his jacket and ran off.

I stared at Marcus's apartments, the lights in his window were still on. I knew he'd be coming home very soon and I knew now that when he returned, I would be waiting.

## Listen

**Elizabeth Ellen**

He's white but he walks like a black man on TV. He struts around our apartment like he's George Jefferson after he fucks my mother. He winks at us and throws his shoulders back and swaggers from one end of the living room to the other like he's in the middle of a ring in Vegas, waiting for the bell to ring. Then he opens a Michelob and lights a Winston and we remember he's not.

I can hear them through my bedroom wall. It's a small apartment and the walls are paper-thin. My bed's a mattress on the floor. I complained to my mother that they're keeping me up at night. She told Mike and he laughed and handed me a pair of earplugs he had sitting on the dashboard of his truck, leftovers from his last construction job. I try shoving them in my ears. I try listening to Madonna real loud on my headphones. I put all three pillows over my head at once, but I can still hear her moaning and telling him to fuck her harder. I can still hear the water in their bed slapping against my wall. They've been together over a year now and they still fuck every night and sometimes on weekend afternoons when I'm supposed to be at the pool. I pray that he'll make her cum quicker so I can get some sleep. I'm tired in the morning when I have to get up and walk to school.

They work afternoons and evenings, so they can sleep in. They wake up slowly and fuck again, then make a pot of coffee and watch *The Beverly Hillbillies*, which is Mike's favorite show. They work together at a bar down the street where the Hell's Angels hang out and I'm not allowed to go. Last Friday night they got arrested and Mom had to call my grandfather back in Ohio and have him wire her bail money. It was in the newspaper. Mike cut out the paragraph pertaining to them and hung it on our refrigerator next to my report card. Mom says they were fighting about something stupid as usual and the manager asked them to take it outside. When they're not fucking, they're fighting. Usually Mom hits first, then Mike hits back, only harder. Maybe this is what she's been looking for all along: someone who will beat her when she's bad, shove her nose in her own shit.

They're both strong from working construction when they first got out here. They had to get up early then because in Arizona it's too hot to work outside in the afternoon. When the cops drove by they were yelling at each other and maybe taking a swing or two. Mom can't remember for sure. They drink while they're working. Sometimes they swallow pills or smoke shit if it's around. Most nights it is, which is probably the main reason we're here if you want to know the truth. They got Mom for resisting arrest. She doesn't like cops; neither of them does. She didn't see what business it was of theirs if she and her man had a little disagreement. They weren't hurting anyone else. She said they never told her she was under arrest so she just started walking down the street. Or maybe she ran. Like I said, it's hard for her to remember. They had to put Mike in a padded cell and keep him overnight. Mom got out after a couple of hours when her father's money arrived. It took Mike all night to calm down.

They met over a year ago when we were still living in Ohio. They met in a bar Mom tended on the nights I made myself macaroni and cheese and tucked myself into bed. The farmhouse we were renting was double the size of most of the other houses we'd lived in and I had my own room upstairs. It'd been four years since the breakup of her last marriage and I had gotten used to having her all to myself again. Sometimes when I woke up in the morning there would be a strange man's voice coming from my mom's room, but it would always be gone by the time I got home from school. Just as soon as you take the time to hope things never change, that's when they surely will.

Right away Mike had plans. Mike wanted to leave town and take Mom with him. He knew people in Arizona. He could get them both jobs. He told Mom how beautiful it was in the West and how different the people there were. He told her she deserved a break. He reminded her that I was fifteen. He said I didn't need my mommy anymore. He told her everything she wanted to hear and then he fucked her hard like she wanted to be fucked. Within a month he had told his daughter goodbye and expected her to do the same.

"I wasn't the one who put you in boarding school," she told me when I walked off the plane last August, twenty pounds heavier, with a scowl on my face. "That was your father's decision. I just wanted you to have a chance to get to know him. You'd been living with me for fifteen years. I thought it was his turn."

When Casey couldn't sleep I would read to her. We'd sit in the dark on opposing beds and wait for Mrs. Stone, our housemother, to pass twice by our door making her nightly rounds. Casey would be cross-legged atop her mattress, clutching her illuminated Glo-worm under her arm and absently fingering an old satin bra that hung between her thumb and forefinger. She did this incessantly without thinking of it whenever she was still—like a small child sucks his thumb or an old woman rubs the arms of her rocking chair—and I envied her these habits, having no good ones of my own. After Mrs. Stone had closed and locked her door, I would pull a book and flashlight from under my bed and begin to read. It was usually something trashy, one of her mother's paperbacks brought from home. *Hollywood Wives* was her favorite and by far the longest. But I didn't mind. I would have read anything, done anything, to make her happy. There were nights I read until my voice was no more than a scratch on the wall. These were the nights she crossed the room to my bed. Anything to keep her nearer me.

It worked out perfectly: Casey's needing me. On nights when her monthly cramps kept her hunched over on her bed, silently soaking her pillow, I would walk her to the bathroom and sit with her as she submerged her body in the warm water. I sat on the edge of the tub in my button-down, broadcloth pajamas and studied the shape of her small breasts, protruding hips and flattened stomach. I told her stories of my mother and listened as she told me ones of her own. We had told them before, many times since that first night alone in our room, but it didn't matter. There was comfort in the telling. We knew that.

It's sort of funny, all the talk in novels and movies and psychology books about the importance of a father in the adolescent girl's life because, honestly, I can't remember Casey ever mentioning hers. None of us did. Then again, none of the Lost Boys or Peter Pan ever asked Wendy to tell them stories of her father. Before you address your wants, you have to first attend to your needs. Fathers felt to us at the academy like luxury items we had no business buying.

She tells him again to fuck her harder and for once I want him to, too. I want him to fuck her so hard she'll bleed for days. I want him to keep fucking her until she can't talk or scream or beg, until all she can do is shut up and sleep. She says Oh God and Oh yeah and Oh Mike and Oh baby and my hand slides up my gown. She pants and yelps and gasps and I'm disgusted and wet and exhausted all at once. I finger myself to the vibration of their movements and ignore the tears as they trickle through my hair.

I chant and cheer him on inside my head. Fuck her, Mike. Harder. Come on, Mike. You can fuck her harder than that. Fuck her like you really mean it, man. Don't be such a pussy. Listen to her. She's screaming for it. Shut her the fuck up.

But he's not listening.

And she screams louder.

Before there was Mike there was Wolfgang. And before Wolfgang left, my biggest fear was tornadoes. I did reports on them for school and hid in the basement with my cat and dog and a Habitrail full of mix-breed gerbils every time a storm blew across the fields. After Wolfgang was gone I forgot all about tornadoes. After Wolfgang split the only thing I feared was my mother. I didn't want to find her in the bathtub with her wrists sliced open or her mouth stuffed with pills. Her bookshelves were full of Sylvia Plath and Virginia Woolf. I knew what could happen.

On the afternoons she didn't get out of bed I walked the floor outside her door, peeking through the crack and listening to her moans, waiting for them to stop so I could rush in and save her. I paid close attention when they demonstrated CPR in school. I took notes and drew diagrams and practiced on the dummy long after everyone else was done. I wanted to be certain to get it right.

I did the laundry and pushed Murphy's Oil soap around the wood floors. I used the mop because my mother wasn't awake to tell me to get down on my knees and use a sponge. I washed my dishes and swept the stairs. My fingers shriveled and smelled like the insides of our bucket and my mother did not die.

This was the summer my mother's friend, Linda, stuck her ex-husband's gun in her mouth and blew her head off. Three weeks later, another friend of hers did the same thing, but instead of blowing her head off, she blinded herself.

Suddenly tornadoes didn't seem that real a threat. We didn't know anyone who had been killed or maimed by a tornado. It got so I didn't even hear the wind in the trees anymore. I was too busy counting my mother's breaths.

The magazine under their bed said to place it in a pan of water on the stovetop and warm it up a bit first. It said if you do this it would feel more lifelike, more like a real dick, when you slide it in. But it's late and they might hear me. I don't want to leave my room. I wouldn't know what a real dick feels like anyway. I'm sixteen and I've yet to have a boy's tongue thrust inside my mouth, let alone his dick. All I know about this shit is what I hear through their walls at night and read in the magazines under their bed when they're gone.

The magazine didn't say anything about size or shape. I stood in the produce section of the grocery store for three minutes on my way home from school, trying to make a decision. It's hard enough to choose a vegetable when all you're going to do with it is eat it. It's even harder when you're planning on shoving it inside yourself and pretending it's a dick. I didn't get the biggest one they had. I thought that might look too obvious. In the end I grabbed a smallish one without too many bumps and threw it in the basket alongside the carrots and red pepper. I wanted it to look like I was making a salad or veggie tray. I didn't want the boy at the counter to know the level of my desperation. I thought I recognized him from my second period health class. I thought he was the one who sat in the back and talked like a surfer.

It's been over an hour and they're still going at it. I reach under the covers and feel around. I hid it down below where it would be warm. It feels funny in my hands and I know that my fingers and insides will smell like produce when I'm done. I will have to scrub myself extra hard in the morning so that I won't be reminded all day of how I molested myself tonight.

Her voice is loud and strong and I wonder if she is ever conscious of it or of me hearing it or of anything at all. She told me once that there's no such thing as a nymphomaniac. She said it's just a word made up and used by men who are afraid of women. She said calling women 'nymphomaniacs' isn't much different than cutting out their clitorises or sewing shut their vaginas. She said the fact that you never hear of a male nymphomaniac ought to be proof enough.

When I was eight or nine and Wolfgang still lived with us I used to think he was hurting her. My mother and he took long naps on weekend afternoons. They would tell me how sleepy they were and that I should be a good girl and play by myself for an hour or two. I'd sit in the room outside theirs, the one they'd designated my playroom, and tend to my dolls. I'd wash and change them and give them a bottle and listen to the strange sounds my mother made. I barely recognized her voice. It sounded throaty and deep, like our cat's before we got her fixed.

Mike, Mike, baby, yeah.

Oh baby yeah.

The cucumber slips inside too easily. I had thought there would be some sort of resistance. I had assumed there would be pain or blood or both. Instead there is neither. I wonder if it's possible I had an accident as a child and my mother never told me. Maybe I fell on my bike and don't remember. That happened to my friend, Heidi. She fell on a gate when she was very little and broke her hymen. Last year when she lost her virginity she claimed it didn't hurt at all. The cucumber doesn't hurt. In fact, it feels sort of comforting, like a favorite blanket or stuffed animal, and I wonder if this is what a real penis feels like. I pull it halfway out and slide it back in. I listen to her affirmations.

Yes. Yes. Yes, she says.

Yes.

She is close. She is finally nearing the end. Soon there will be quiet. Soon we all will sleep.

The cucumber takes on a motion of its own, propelled by her insistences, and my hand rushes to keep up. I read once in a magazine that it's not uncommon for rape victims to experience orgasm during the rape. But this fact is of little comfort. She makes a final, guttural moan. It seems without end. It seems as though it will go on and on and on and then, finally, without warning, it stops and there is nothingness. The wall is silent, my hand falls to my side, and all I can feel is my heartbeat, in places it's never been before.

I wait for it to slow down, then tiptoe into the kitchen and bury the evidence beneath the potato peelings and eggshells from dinner. Mike likes to make us potato pancakes on the nights they're off work. He puts applesauce on his and we eat ours plain or with sour cream. Mike let me peel the potatoes. He stood behind me at the counter and showed me how to hold the peeler so I wouldn't slice off my fingers. He smelled a little bit like radishes and a little bit like the beer cans and cigarette butts I throw away each morning. I make sure to bury it deep down where he won't see. I don't want him to know what kind of girl I am. I don't want him to think I'm like her.

His daughter's school picture hangs on our fridge. She's the same age as me and I wonder how many minutes of her day she spends thinking of her dad. I wonder if she ever asks her mother to tell her stories about him. I study her face. It's pink and round and I doubt she's ever snuck a vegetable into her bedroom at night. She's not like us.

I go back to my room and fold myself onto my mattress. I bury my head beneath my pillow. I won't want to get up in the morning. It will burn when I pee and the water in the shower won't ever get hot enough.

I listen for the wind but there is only stillness. I had forgotten for a second where we are. Here in Arizona, children don't know to fear tornadoes. At school we practice only fire safety. We don't crouch down under our desks with our arms over our heads when the bell rings. Instead we walk swiftly to the nearest exit and stand in groups of twos and threes on the school lawn, waiting for our teachers to tell us it's safe to go back inside. I want to tell them they're wasting their time. No one we know has ever died in a fire.

Good girls listen to their mothers. I am never not listening to mine. I listen to her moan when Mike fucks her and I listen to her scream when he hits her. I listen as she cries when he threatens to leave. I listen as she begs him to stay. It's quiet now, but one night Mike will leave. They all leave, eventually. And when that time comes, I will listen once more for her breaths. I will stand outside her door and count them. I will wait for her to need me.

## The Lady with the Mannequin Arm

**Davy Rothbart**

My grandmother lives in a sprawling retirement community outside Fort Lauderdale called Wynmoor Village. For three months in 1999, after my grandpa died, I lived there, too. It was an adventure of sorts.

My grandmother was pretty lonely and down and she and I had always got along real well, so I figured I'd go stay with her and give her some company, and also escape from winter for a while. There's a big difference between getting along with your grandmother to actually moving in and living together. But things started off pretty well and we got into a good routine. I turned the study into a little bedroom and she was amazingly cool about letting me keep my own hours. I'd stay up really late writing and reading and go to sleep around 6 a.m., then sleep till one in the afternoon. I'd eat breakfast while she ate lunch, then we'd hang out around the little pool shared by her building and the neighboring building—we'd play backgammon or talk or read. Then we'd have an early dinner, I'd drive to the park to play basketball for a couple hours, come home, and start the night of work. She'd watch TV till midnight or so and then come in to say goodnight. My grandmother is amazing, one of those old people who you can really communicate with, who responds with clarity and wit, and who isn't shocked by anything. I knew she was hurting but she didn't like to talk too much about my grandpa. Sometimes she'd sock herself in her room with the Home Shopping Network booming. Then other times she would talk merrily on the phone to her friends.

Wynmoor Village is huge, a whole gated town. Some days I'd jog a mile to the main pool and fitness center. I'd never done weight training before but I kinda got into it, pumping iron while the easy-listening station cranked out songs from *Dirty Dancing* over a pair of tinny loudspeakers. The three or four wiry, rugged-looking old-timers who hung out there intimidated me at first but then began to sweetly give me pointers on how to do sit-ups correctly, and lat-pulls. Walking back to the apartment, red and yellow birds flapped everywhere and cars rolled by at ten-miles-an-hour on the wide Wynmoor Village thoroughfares. It's such a strange, controlled environment, but it was weird how quickly I got used to the mildness and hush of everything. When I left to play basketball or get groceries, everything beyond Wynmoor's gates felt overstimulating, harsh, cacophonous. It was only ten miles to the ocean but I hardly ever went—better to hang out by the pool.

The second week I was there I met Virgil, the guy in the apartment next door. He was 91 years old. His nose was bright red from decades of hard drinking, and he wore a pirate patch over his right eye (though he told me many stories over the next three months, he never told me how he'd lost his eye). Virgil was the kind of drinker who likes company to drink, and he'd invite me over in the afternoons, tell long stories and force me to match him drink for drink. By the time I got out of there a couple hours later I was always rocked. I'd be fumbling plates and tipping candles trying to set the table for my grandma and me to have dinner.

"You shouldn't let Virgil bully you into anything," my grandma would say.

In return, I'd bounce around the kitchen and shout, "Dinner smells delicious! Yeah, boyeeee, let's get our grub on, Grand-mama!"

I was having trouble getting any writing done, so I started going back to Virgil's place at night, too, after I got back from basketball. His liquor cabinet was gigantic. He'd bring down a strangely-shaped brown bottle and say things like, "Try this one, it'll put hair on your chest."

Most of his stories were about his childhood in New York and his experiences in World War II in Europe. His unit was in Spain and Portugal and never saw combat. Instead they fought each other and the locals. His best friend was killed trying to jump a horse across a deep crevasse. His friend hopped on the horse and raced toward the gully, and at the edge the horse balked and his friend tumbled in. There had been money on whether or not they'd get across. Virgil actually won money on his friend's death. He said he won a lot of money in Lisbon betting on stunts like this and he sent the money home to his sister who used it to open a hat shop, which still existed under the same name fifty years later, though now it was owned by Nigerians.

At some point, sometimes mid-story, or even mid-sentence, Virgil would stand and disappear into a back room as though he was going to take a leak, but he wouldn't reappear. I'd sit there for a few minutes, waiting for him to come back. I'd finish my drink, gaze around the room for a while, maybe reach out and touch the texture of some of the various bottles that had moved from the cabinet to the table we sat at, and then finally I'd let myself out and go back to my grandma's apartment where the Home Shopping Network was rumbling and every painting and bowl of seashells in the place seemed like the saddest thing on earth.

My grandpa, we went to visit him two years before, a few months before he died—my mom, me, and my little brother. My grandpa had been deteriorating from Parkinson's for years, but things had gotten worse and we understood that this was the last time we'd see him alive. We watched a basketball game together on the little TV in the bedroom. Then my grandpa said he wanted to talk to me alone. The medication had him in a bad state and you had to get very close to make out his words. He told me that he'd been trying to figure out why God was punishing him with this disease, and that the only thing he could think of was that it was punishment for the fact that he hadn't insisted that me and my brothers get Bar Mitzvah'd. I told him I thought that was bullshit, that it wasn't punishment for anything, it was just a disease. But he was certain. He pointed with his eyes toward a series of tomes on his bookshelf—a 15-book set called *The History of Judaism*. He told me his last wish was that I'd read it and learn the history of our people. What could I say? I told him I would.

When I was living there, sometimes I'd take a peek at those books and even take one down to the pool in the afternoon and make an earnest attempt to start reading, but I'd never get past page six. This other guy from the building named Mark would play backgammon with my grandma while I sat on one of the twangy deck recliners with the big tomes in my lap. I'd lay there with my eyes closed and listen to their small talk. Mark was kind and liked to tell jokes. His wife had died after a long illness a few years before. Whenever Mark talked about my grandpa he called him Jay, which was weird to me because I'd never heard anyone call him by his name, they all called him Pa. Mark and him had been friends. Mark and my grandma talked and talked, then they'd lapse into silence and there'd be only the sound of dice rolling and backgammon tiles clicking against each other, and maybe, distantly, a sound from the outside world, from the high school that was nestled against Wynmoor's walls—a car door slamming shut, a kid's shout. I'd drift off, and when I woke up eighty minutes later the big *History of Judaism* tome would've left a white square on my belly where it had blocked the sun.

One night in April—it was the night before my birthday, actually—Virgil and I had a long, late session. He was recklessly drunk. I'd been alternating between liquor and Slice, which is like Sprite. But I was still feeling the liquor. It got very late. Then suddenly I broke open or something. For all the stories Virgil had told me, I hadn't told him one thing about my life—not because I didn't think he'd be interested, but more because I liked his stories and didn't feel like telling ones I already knew. But suddenly everything came pouring out of me. I told him how my grandpa had made me promise to read those books and how I was letting him down. I told him about having my heart broken in Scotland and how I was still in love with the girl years later. And the story of the last time I'd seen her, flying a hot-air balloon and crash-landing it. I told him about stupid shit, like the day in sixth grade when David Pfeifer beat me up with a pair of nunchuks, and I even told him about the decades-old *Young Students' Encyclopedia* I'd found in the fitness center that day: Volume 14, Negro to Pantomime. The fact that I was living so far from the world I'd known bore down on me like a great weight. I felt as old as Virgil, and anything that had happened in my life before Wynmoor seemed distantly in the past. I felt like a man on his deathbed reviewing his life. I couldn't stop telling stories, and Virgil sat there nodding and gnawing on ice cubes and fingering his eye patch and pouring himself drinks.

Then, out of nowhere, a woman appeared in the doorway to the back hallway. I was startled into complete silence. She looked to be in her seventies or eighties, and she had on a long lavender nightgown.

"Come to bed, Virgil," she said.

She smiled at me like a ghost might smile at someone who couldn't see them. She moved closer, right beside the table, and I realized a strange thing: one of her arms, the one dangling right in front of me, was a dark arm, and it was not real. It looked like it was made of brown porcelain. It was completely straight, and hung from her shoulder like a golf club. I wanted to touch it. Who was this woman? This whole time—three months almost—I'd had no idea Virgil was married. Was this his wife? And why had someone stripped an African-American mannequin of its arm and mounted it on this old woman? What had happened to her real arm? And where, for that matter, was Virgil's right eye? Really, wasn't that the story I'd been waiting for all these hot late nights, wasn't that the obvious riddle, the hook which had me coming back for more rum and gin and scotch again and again? Of course, I realized, Virgil knew this, and that's why he'd kept me in suspense—he didn't want to lose his drinking partner. The woman turned and headed back through the doorway; as she turned the corner her stiff arm brushed the doorframe and made a soft clunk. Virgil stood and followed her. I sat at the table touching the bottles.

Then I whirled out of there and back to my grandma's place. Heavy Home Shopping Network bass thundered out from under her door. I rushed right up to her door and raised my hand to rap on it, but paused. The night felt tilted and wild. Finally I barged right in. Her bed was empty. In the light from the TV I could see a little. The sheets were thrown back and the remote was on top of the covers. She had her own bathroom and I thought maybe she was in her bathroom but she wasn't. I went to her window, which looked out on the pool. All the deck furniture had been carefully arranged by the maintenance staff and glowed orange under tall lamps here and there. Then I saw them, standing still and very close together in one corner of the shallow end, underwater lights casting them in eerie, moving shadows—my grandma and Mark. They were a ways away, maybe a hundred feet, and it took a few moments for me to see what they were doing, and to understand that they were kissing. They were touching each other's faces with their hands. It was breathtaking. My heart blasted away.

Next — and this seemed to make sense at the time — I raced out of her room and to the study (my room) and grabbed one of the big *History of Judaism* tomes and my keys, then grabbed a stack of six beach towels from the hallway closet and headed for the door. Halfway out, I wheeled around and went back to my grandma's room and took up the remote and changed the channel one channel down, which happened to be, I discovered, Nickelodeon. I left again, went to my car, drifted through the silent, smooth Wynmoor streets and out the west gate, and drove fifteen minutes to the beach.

I stretched out in the cool sand, twenty feet from the water, and covered myself in towels. The ocean gathered itself and crashed mightily onto shore. All the stars were sparkling. I pulled out the big *History of Judaism* tome and realized I'd grabbed the wrong book—what I'd actually grabbed was the encyclopedia I'd found that day: Volume 14, Negro to Pantomime. I held it in my arms and watched the ocean. Its power and majesty was utterly captivating. The tides took deep inward breaths and then unleashed themselves, and every time the surf pounded down I felt the jolt in the sand beneath me. It was warm and windy. Portugal was somewhere out there. So was Scotland. I hunkered down in my towels. I guess I fell asleep, because a couple hours later I woke up to a purple dawn, and the ocean was absolutely calm. Over the course of an hour I watched the most beautiful understated transition from night to day, as the sky changed from dark purple to dark blue to dark red to red, then to orange to yellow and to pink—and still the sun had not yet come up. A big white gull landed close by and we watched together as the sun broke over the edge of the horizon, red and searing, at which point the gull batted its wings and cried out twice, each cry in two beats, like the words Hap-py and Birth-day.

## Call Waiting

**Jonathan Lethem**

My best friend Philip lives across the country, in New England. Two or three times a week we talk on the telephone, late into the night. The bills are enormous. I've only seen Philip in the flesh twice in the last seven years, and it was a shock both times. His head and face seemed huge. His whole body seemed huge. For me, Philip is a voice. Whining, cajoling, insouciant, but always a voice in my ear. Or a laugh.

It's great to see Philip, but it also bugs me to see the voice and laugh embodied in a lug who takes out the garbage and makes eggs for his girlfriend.

Philip is a musician. He plays the college-town-bar circuit; he's good. I'm a science fiction writer. Philip and I are both mostly about ourselves.

One night, in the middle of our cackling over some old, old joke, his phone clicks: call waiting. His. I never mistake his for mine anymore.

"Be right back," he said, and clicked away.

So I was thrust into that twilight realm, that modern undeath. I'm only partly kidding. I sit in the dark, the room lit only by my computer screen and the power indicators on the stacked components of my stereo. Through the windows of my lonely apartment I can see other apartment windows, and hear a trace of street noise. These cursors blinked at me, sketching a possible environment, but I'm not here, I'm not home. When I'm talking to Philip my voice and my consciousness have turned away from my real life in California, and tunneled electronically to New Hampshire. Call waiting is a strange variant, then; I've gone all that way, I'm residing in Philip's phone, I'm still nestled beside his head, but I've been shunted into some vacant side space.

It's like inviting someone to journey a great distance to visit you and then putting them in a sensory deprivation chamber.

So I hovered there—infinite, distended—until Philip came back. "Who was that?" I said.

"This girl," he said. Philip and I are both over 30; it shouldn't be a girl anymore. But anyway.

"What girl?" I said. "You have a girlfriend."

"I know, it's not anything. She was my opening act last week."

"Good?" I asked.

"She's talented. Really young, but smart. Kind of folky, singer-songwriter corny at the moment. But she could be another Liz Phair or Ani DiFranco. Or... I don't know. I'm no judge."

Philip works at a record store, too, and he's always up on the latest. I didn't even know who Liz Phair or Ani DiFranco were. But young and smart, and the interest I detected in Philip's voice, was enough. I was in love.

I didn't have a girlfriend.

Philip and I slept with several of the same women back at college. Four, actually, which is a lot. The first two concurrences tested our friendship, but by the fourth it was a big comradely joke between us. Even the homoerotic subtext, which the women tended to want to point out to us, got incorporated. So I knew his taste pretty well.

"You have a girlfriend," I said. "What are you doing?"

"Nothing, talking."

Wrong, I thought. I'd been the one doing nothing. Nothing and talking weren't the same: thus, call waiting.

"It's kind of intimate, actually," I said. "Being on call waiting with a strange and attractive woman. It's cozy, two of us in your phone together, side by side, but with this invisible barrier. Your phone put us into the same tiny little space together, even though I don't know her number or even her name."

"I can see what you mean," said Philip.

"Did you describe me to her? Did she ask who was on the other line?"

"My well-hung, Nobel-winning friend. Of course."

"No, really."

"I just said, 'My friend.' "

"Good. Leave it at that for now."

And we went on to other things. But two nights later she interrupted us again. I felt sure it was her even before Philip came back.

He confirmed my intuition, and I said, "I want to be on call waiting with her as much as possible."

"This sounds serious, " said Philip.

"I think I'm in love."

"You just haven't been that close to anyone for a long time. It's a desert island thing. You should get out more."

"No, it's her."

"You want her number?"

"No."

I'm a science fiction writer. So I understood it as a romance across a void of realms and dimensions. Classic pulp heartbreak: The Girl From Alternate Earth. You Can Love Her But You Can Never Have Her.

Philip humored me. "I told her I'd call her back after I got off with you," he said. "If you want, you can call me in the middle of that."

"Yes. That's good. Only let it ring a few times, like you're not sure you want to bother. Like you're annoyed with call waiting. Then finally get it after five or six rings. I want to feel myself interrupting her call, I want to savor that."

"Okay. And then when I pick you up, she'll be the one on hold for you. It's the equivalent of being 'on top'."

"Yes."

Twenty minutes later I was ringing Philip's line. I felt surprisingly nervous. Six rings, and he picked up.

"Is she there?" I whispered.

"Yes. But she's kind of impatient. She's getting sick of call waiting."

I swallowed. "Keep her there for a minute, okay?"

"No problem. She'll wait."

"Why do you say that like that?"

"Like what?"

"The way you said it: 'She'll wait.' What's going on with you two?"

"Nothing."

"Are you flirting? It's okay if you are, I just want to know. I'm not jealous. That's the nature of this kind of thing, the kind of relationship she and I are having, the call waiting type of affair. You can't be jealous."

"We're flirting."

"That's good, that's okay. What's going to happen?"

"Nothing. Nothing real. I'm with Cynthia, you know that."

"Nothing real?"

"I don't know," said Philip. " We might have phone sex."

Phone sex! Philip astonished me. His ability to perform on the phone, to mingle voices with a real person, was far beyond me. Perhaps it had something to do with his musical talent. I'd once called a sex number from the back pages of the *East Bay Express* and been paralyzed, mute, as a bored woman sucked her finger and talked me through a generic blowjob fantasy.

Philip had done this sort of thing once before, had a phone sex affair with a friend. Afterwards, with me, he was somber and regretful. We'd discussed the question of whether or not it was a betrayal of Cynthia, but couldn't decide. Such an obvious question, but all we could do was pose it and then lapse into cowed, glum silence.

Someone once defined the job of a science fiction writer—generously, I think—as working out in advance the human problems that come with technological change. It sounds good. Yet I couldn't even grapple with the ethics of the telephone! So what was science fiction for?

"Phone sex? Really?" I said to Philip now. "Can I be on call waiting?"

"Of course. Listen, I'd better get back now. How is it for you, being on top? Having her on hold?"

"Well, it's okay. But I don't like doing this to her. I want to be the invisible one; I want to creep around the marginal spaces. She should always be alive, connected, talking, that's the way I want to think of her."

"I understand," said Philip. I knew he did. "So stay on when I switch back to her. Stay as long as you like."

"What if you hang up? And I'm nowhere."

"I think if I hang up, you'll be cut off. We're going to talk awhile, anyway."

"Are you going to have phone sex now?"

"I don't know."

"So she might be coming, over the phone, while I'm right there on call waiting?"

"Maybe."

"Wow. Okay, go. I can't stand to think about it anymore."

Then I was alone, a proximate phantom. The silence on the line was plush and I fell into it. This was anything but emptiness; I could feel her there, and feel myself close to her. I was invisible, though. I was the purloined letter. I was just an ache close to her heart.

I had an erection, so I masturbated. It made me feel even closer to her. I didn't even know her name.

Three days passed before I spoke to Philip again. "Did you have phone sex?" I asked.

"With who?" he deadpanned.

"Three nights ago."

"Oh, that. I didn't think you believed me. I made her up. It was a call from Cynthia, then a call from my manager, whatever. There was no girl."

"No girl?"

"Nope."

I'm a science fiction writer; I can deal with abrupt disjunctions. I was defiant. I concluded that she existed, whether Philip knew her or not. A young smart folky-corny talented singer, like Liz Phair or Ani DiFranco. Philip was joking, but I wasn't. I would find the girl whose existence he'd extrapolated. She had to be somewhere. And then what? Call her?

I must have been silent for a long time, because Philip said, "I'm kidding."

"She's real?" I shouldn't have been surprised. It made sense that Philip was feeling a little guilty towards Cynthia. The jokey equivocation was a cover; he'd done something he regretted.

"Yes," he said. "But there's something you should know."

"What?"

"She's already... how can I put this? She's got this guy and they—"

"That doesn't matter."

"No, listen. She's already got this call waiting thing going with this other guy. He's already filling her 'call waiting needs', so to speak."

Then Philip started laughing.

"Fuck you," I said.

We changed the subject, but it was too late. I'd experienced a loss. I felt it in my chest, like I'd swallowed my telephone. Suddenly there was no going back to what I'd had, to what she and I had shared.

I didn't say anything about it to Philip.

When I got off the phone, I unplugged it. That night I started a new story, about an astronaut and a woman he glimpses inside a passing black hole, and how They Can Never Be Together But They Will Love One Another Until The End Of Time.

## Basic Rules for Handling Your Shotgun[1]

T. Cooper

I'd taken my clothes off, all of them, in the cold restroom of the trailer park just beside I-90 there, where it all ends as far as the West is concerned. I needed a shower bad, and could overlook the overflowing toilet in stall number one and moldy-black curtain in shower stall two. My dirty clothes sloughed off me into a pile on the yellow tile floor. Its grout boasted years of bleach and grime and probably tears. I hung my towel on the loose brass hook and gave the hot water a chance to wake up.

I stepped into the modest trickle of water then, which was surprisingly warm and understanding. But as soon as I registered the slightest sliver of comfort, my foot sent an urgent message that something was wrong: I'd stepped in shit, and two full spaces between my first three toes were full of it. I couldn't immediately determine for certain the type of creature that had created it: animal or human? It seemed human.

I managed to get a $15 refund from the smoke-stained clerk in the front office and then proceeded to drive our rig out of that park with alacrity. [Think of an ambulance-type of van that's been converted into a real first-rate, aerodynamic Recreational Vehicle—not the ungainly, boxy type of wind-dragger you see in the slow lane, with wavy patterns in every shade of brown known to nature splashed along the side.] Every time I applied the brake, or accelerated—every step thereafter that day, even in the 7-Eleven, where the only consolation at 8 a.m. after wedging shit between your toes is a Coke Slurpee (and that barely does it)—I simply couldn't dispense of the sensation of shit stuck to my foot. Standing naked in the shower on the unaffected foot, I'd been helpless. Kicking didn't help. Nor flicking. I needed a paper towel, and none available, I went for the troublingly thin toilet paper. My traveling companion, in the shower stall next to my own, just watched me and gagged, both audibly and visibly, as I hopped around the room in front of her.

And for some reason still unknown to me, and fully inexplicable outside of the general condition of shock, I picked up the rest of the feces of questionable origin from the shower floor with the little toilet paper I had left, and tossed it all into the trash before exiting the bathroom.

After we exited the Kamper King RV-Trailer Park and Aquatic Center and pulled onto the road, she said:

—Why does this hurt me more than it hurts you, when it's you who feels the actual pain? [My companion was apparently more traumatized, scarred irrevocably even, by the incident than myself. Or to be fair, she might've been talking about something else entirely.]

—I can still feel it through my shoe, in my sock. I'm haunted by the phantom. Not you.

—But I had to watch.

—Yeah? Well, then you drive.

—I knew there was something wrong with that place when we pulled in there.

1. Always treat every shotgun as if it were loaded.

When you pull into a trailer park after 8 or 9 p.m., you have to night-register. It is late and the office is closed, and there is a handwritten, usually faded sign directing you to find a spot for your rig, plug in, and check in first thing in the morning. First thing. So you find a space, plug in, and pay in the morning. But as you drive up, even though it's supposed to be closed, polyester curtains get drawn back in trailers all around, and you can't see because it's dark inside them, but usually four eyes scrutinize first you, then the make and model of your rig, and finally how you maneuver around the tight lot, and whether you take your small dog to the designated pet area or just let it do its business just once because it's late, because no one's watching, on the fence or up against a Rubbermaid trash bin belonging to a resident of the park who's a little more permanent than yourself.

When you are new to this, hell, new to so many things, but especially this. When you look like a no-account rap star because your clothes are too big, and it's cold and the hooded sweatshirt you're sporting is actually for warmth. When you are short but look like you should be a man, but have the small thin fingers of a teenaged boy or even a woman. And your traveling companion is a tall and slender, beautiful girl who you have no business getting, much less having. When all these things are the case:

You do not go up to someone else's hook-up post with a flashlight, *just to see how they do it.* There are three sockets with different numbers and amps and voltages on your post, and you think because of the rain the chances for accidental electrocution are higher, can only be exponentially higher, because there are three of them. You can't remember the saying about 'cut off the finger to spite the hand,' or 'in spite of the hand,' but it's coming to you. Just try all of the sockets on your own post first, even though it's the Pacific Northwest and it's of course raining and the process of elimination was one of the first things you learned in science class as a viable method for accomplishing things. But this time it doesn't work, the trusty process, and you try the same thing over and over again without eliminating it. So you just tiptoe over to the post across the way, connected via a thick black rubber water hose and a few green electrical cords to a long white trailer with obvious and ancient ties to the land.

2. NEVER, EVER, POINT ANY SHOTGUN, LOADED OR UNLOADED, AT ANYTHING YOU DO NOT INTEND TO SHOOT.

"Hold on a goddamn minute!"

"Oh."

"Now, son, you just put those hands up where I can see them, and everything's gonna be okay here."

[The cover to the electrical box on his hook-up cracks the bridge of your nose on its way back down, but in the rain and with a shiny shotgun barrel poking out of the side door of a slide-in Holiday Rambler Presidential series trailer, it doesn't hurt one bit. You can just make out a bead of blood—a black blur to your eyes—as it washes down one side of your nose on a drop of rain.]

"What do you think you're doin', fella?"

"I just pulled in and the office is closed, and I didn't know how to hook up, so I thought I'd just take a look at yours."

"What number?"

"I thought it was 30 amps but then I saw the 50 and—"

"No, what site did you pull in to?"

"To be honest, we just pulled in and it's dark and I just don't know."

"That's the first thing you know."

"—"

"You know the number."

"I know, but I don't know it."

"You're not gonna find anything snooping around here, fella. We don't have anything for you."

"I'm really not snooping, sir. Honest."

[I did not live through everything just to get mowed down by some wingnut with an assault weapon purportedly used for hunting game. Not for this shit.]

"Now what's gonna happen is you're gonna turn around and march on out of here and I'll watch you the whole time, and if you don't turn back, I'm not gonna alert the authorities. Or dump some of this lead in your skinny rear."

3. KEEP YOUR FINGER OFF THE TRIGGER UNTIL YOU ARE ACTUALLY AIMING AT THE TARGET AND READY TO SHOOT.

As God as my witness, the sign when you drive in to this place reads, "Howdy, Pardner." We'd chuckled in our self-satisfied manner at that on the way in. But then we noticed even bigger, below "Howdy, Pardner," was "Welcome... and We mean IT!" Marching out backwards the way I came in, only on foot with my arms sticking up, a shotgun barrel behind me, and without four tons of steel as my shepherd, I am decidedly less welcome than I was when I first passed these parts. Pardner.

I do this sometimes. Like the time when Melanie Cosgrove promised to give me a professional Swedish massage (it was big that year), and I made her promise not to look in front, at the ropy red line running the length of my torso they said would fade as I grew older. "Just my back," I made her promise. But under the pecan tree in the shade in the grass, three other girls in our grade, plus two fifth graders, were watching. And when I sat up so Melanie could get a better position, there they all were, laughing and pointing at me over the square-cut row of hedges. I trust people with flawless faces. I switched schools after that, or just didn't go any longer, I can't remember which.

4. THE SAFETY IS ONLY A MECHANICAL DEVICE, NOT A SUBSTITUTE FOR GOOD SENSE.

—Where the hell have you been?

—Are you fucking kidding me, you didn't see that out there?

—What? You forgot to turn on the propane. I have no flame in here.

—You didn't fucking see that whole fucking thing?

—What? The flame?

5. TREAT THE SHOTGUN AS A PRECISION INSTRUMENT.

The next morning at registration. "What kind of rig you got?"

"I don't know, it's not that long, kind of medium length."

"Two adults, and I saw a dog. Looks under twenty pounds, so that's five extra. You're not letting it do its business in the park, are you?"

"No."

"Because there's a designated pet area just out front."

"I know."

"Twenty-seven dollars plus tax."

"For one night?"

Nod.

"Well—"

"What?"

"Is the pool free?"

"Just gotta sign in. Date of birth, too."

"But it's free."

"Sure."

In the pool house the tiles drip a symphony, but here in this barn that is also a pool, you can just make out a slow, merciless '30s blues riff in the drops. How much it hurts, but not the kind of hurt you can see or name.

A portly man with at least a dozen green-black tattoos, a ZZ Top beard, and, I swear, the hairiest back not on a canid, treads water in three and a half feet of yellow water, his long facial mane swishing back and forth gently in front of him. His toes look to be nicking the floor of the pool, but you never know.

"The sauna runs a quarter for fifteen minutes, the Jacuzzi'll take any silver but the new dollar, but if you pop in three quarters you'll get bubbles and jets for half an hour, but no heat."

"—"

"You're from last night, huh? Sorry 'bout that. My bitch wife got spooked when she saw you snooping around. That your little Roadtrek 1600 out there? Nice little rig."

"It does okay."

"Wanna do some laps?"

"I don't know."

"Suit yourself."

I've got skinny legs, not much in the way of stubble, and only two tattoos, but after just twenty minutes, Bruce is my friend. He has six known or acknowledged children, but only one boy out of the whole damn lot. Brewster. Bruce slipped that name onto the birth certificate as homage to himself, phonetically speaking, but he's no poet. He used to make an honest living. Wasn't that clever? It was, I admit, phonetically speaking.

He says Brewster owns a shop and "knows his way around a mower like those camel jockeys know shortcuts in the pyramids." Arabs are on everybody's minds these days.

"I didn't know they have shortcuts in the pyramids."

"Oh yeah. Tons. That's where they hid all the gold. Where do you think we got the idea for secret tunnels in Washington?"

"State?"

"No, the District. Tons of them, tunnels all connecting the Capitol, White House, all underground there in the, uh, tunnels. You know, like King Tut."

"I didn't know that."

"Yeah, well, I heard about it when I was in the service."

"Oh."

"Brewster works on Deeres, but he knows the Jap models, too. He can do a whole transmission himself in two days."

6. OLD OR RELOADED AMMO MAY BE DANGEROUS. WE RECOMMEND AGAINST USING IT.

Later that night, our second in the park, the night before the shit: When I'm out switching on the propane and my beautiful companion's silhouette moves from the front to the middle of the rig, the whole damn thing moves with her. Just her 130 pounds sways those four tons, but to be honest I've seen more than that moved by lesser women. So it's not just a teenaged metaphor for action in a backseat: When this van's a-rockin', don't come a-knockin'.

[*Why she loves me I hope never to comprehend entirely.*]

Later still that night, when we get to some rockin' of our own in the queen-sized fold-out converted bed in the back of the van, I know at 11:08 it's too late for anyone to discern what's going on in the Roadtrek 1600 in site number 12.

—That was hot. I came really hard. Goodnight.

—Don't you want to watch local news with me? We get it. Like, three channels from Seattle.

—You're very sweet. But goodnight.

[*She is done with me, for now. Just for seven hours. I'm getting better at this.*]

There's a massive, ghostly satellite dish forest on the small grassy knoll just east of the trailer park. I walked the dog through it the day before. I wonder whether it has something to do with the tremendous reception this little TV commands, with no antenna to speak of. The dishes are bright white and clean and don't seem abandoned like most of those you pass on the road do.

I am exhaling the bass line for "Another One Bites the Dust" in rhythm with her breathing next to me. It's that steady. She's perfect. But soon there is yelling that interrupts my song and even drowns out the goofy local weatherman with a transparent, invented, weather-related surname: "Austin Raines." He's probably not even from Texas.

"The thing is, we never do go into town. We never pull up stakes and just go." A woman's hysterical, half-crying voice floats across the row toward us. It comes and goes, but mostly comes. And loud. Everything this woman is seems to fly in the face of the quiet-after-10 p.m. rule. Pretty much no one breaks that one. You just don't.

"Say something, you bastard." She is shrieking, and I am scared for myself. And then for her. Just an old reflex. And just for three seconds. "Say something about pulling up the stakes. Just once more, I want to hear it again with the stakes."

"—"

"You pussy," she continues, and I must look. So I push up the polyester curtain above my head, half-expecting a wet, stringy-haired demon's face to be pressed up against the window when I do. But I am relieved to see nothing but the swinging lamp over the row between our van and the trailer across the way, and though it's black out, I feel like I can see everything. The wind causes the less stable things to sway gently: the lamp, a few American flags, sometimes our van. A few pieces of trash swirl by.

A dog barks, but it is not ours.

Then finally: "Shut. The. Fuck. *Up*." A tinny door slams open, and it is the same one through which the rifle was aimed my way just one night before. He is stomping around outside and beneath the slide of their trailer, hands flailing.

I extinguish the TV as quickly as a joint when Mom comes into your bedroom. ["You have so many strikes against you already, why would you make it worse for your poor little body, that beleaguered heart? It just breaks, well, *my* heart."] Beleaguered? *Did the cardiologist teach you that word, Ma? Huh?*

I gently pop the pop-out window and press my ear up against the one-inch opening; it's cold out. I look back to what I've got inside, and notice that all 130 pounds of her are still sleeping beside me, sheets stuck to her thigh. I hear another slam outside and then a fishing rod and reel sail out the same door and through the dark. The door could be comprised of aluminum foil wrapped around plywood as it bounces against the side of the trailer and then slams shut again. It probably is aluminum foil and plywood.

"I sold my motherfucking dream house to wetbacks for this thing so you could see the fucking world!" He is retrieving a very broken-looking fly rod and reel from the hood of a neighbor's hatchback.

"Then let's see it."

"We are. We are seeing it."

"The Sound is twenty miles away, Bruce, and I've never seen it. I want to see the Sound."

"Brewster's working on the Pacer. Give him another week, huh?"

There is silence again. And then: "Oh, Baby Boy."

I'm still stretching to see across the park, but nothing comes for some time. It seems even darker now, the running lights marking a trail to the showers have been extinguished. Now they too are closed for the night. The lamp illuminating the "Howdy Pardner" sign reveals that the skies are once again spitting down on us and into the yellow-purple night. Are there familiar fingers running through greasy, thin and flake-filled hair over there now? Cracked and weary thumbs tracing the same old blurry tattoos? Something as expected as tears?

"Baby, Brewster's not working on the Pacer. We dumped the Pacer."

"We don't have a Pacer? What happened to the Pacer?"

"It's gone."

"I didn't sell the house either."

"No."

"What happened to the house?"

"—"

"We can go into town tomorrow. I promise, we can see the Needle. You'd like that, wouldn't you?"

"I'd like to see the Needle. But it's okay, Baby. We don't have to see it tomorrow. We've got loads of time to see the Needle."

7. IF A SHOTGUN FAILS TO FIRE WHEN THE TRIGGER IS PULLED, KEEP IT POINTED AT THE TARGET FOR AT LEAST 30 SECONDS. SOMETIMES, SLOW PRIMER IGNITION WILL CAUSE A "HANG" FIRE, AND THE CARTRIDGE WILL GO OFF AFTER A SHORT PAUSE.

My mother insists that it is she who gave me my heart. I believe it takes two to do something like that, but she would never be moved. I lay back down to catch up with the steady rhythm of her breathing again next to me, but just as I figure it out, I can't remember what song I'd been exhaling along with her.

I don't sleep because even the headlights going by on I-90, darting across the concave ceiling of the van, are infinitely more encouraging than any dream I may have. When she wakes up there next to me one more time, it will confirm once again that my mother is wrong about almost everything. Has gotten everything wrong since the first time they cracked me open and brought me back.

I could turn the local channels back on and surf all three, but I don't take solace in such variety on this night. Tonight I think I could sleep, and whether or not I actually do, I know it feels like I can, and that is enough.

It's dead silent in the park, and that is why, after I hear that aluminum door close one last time, I can just barely make out the inevitable, surprised choking bursts that come from one in a long lineage of men who weep by the close of each beautiful day.

I shut my eyes and sing.

---

[1] Rules excerpted from public service document by Tayabally, Abdoolally & Sons (oldest arms and ammunition dealer in Pakistan).

## Gymkhana

**Monica Drake**

In college, right away I learned the best way to hit on a guy is to hold his hand if you know him at all. It's that easy. Pick one, and walk beside him as he cuts across the broad, open campus of overly-kept grass or the sweep of psychedelic mushrooms on the football field. Wrap your arm through his. This'll make him nervous but he won't want to show it. Act like the hand holding, the arm wrap, is normal; it's not far off anyway. Ask him a question, and look into his eyes when he answers. Laugh when you can. He'll follow you anywhere.

The night I figured it out I'd been snorting coke with my new roommate, Kyra. New to the dorms, new to snorting coke, bumped up a grade in high school, I was the youngest in college and worst of all, a virgin, getting older by the minute. I didn't want Kyra to know about the virgin part. Still, I told her myself right after that first cool trickle numbed the back of my throat.

I was an outsider in a school of experience. A scholarship student in a world of money.

Kyra said, "Get rid of it," meaning the virginity. She looked down, and cut lines in a way I'd never be able to, fast and sure. A razor in her fingers. I couldn't even shave my legs without nicks. She sat on the window ledge sleek as a cat, in her French-cut cotton Calvin Klein's.

Kyra's theory, she told me the first day, was that people shouldn't wear clothes. "Without clothes," she said, "nobody would get as fat. Who could stand to eat when they see sweat in the creases of their own fat stomach?"

Kyra's stomach was flat and tan, with a long torso. Her hips were low and narrow. The only job she'd ever held, she said, was training polo ponies, riding muscled horses, teaching the animals tricks. Kyra's father was a corporate lawyer, a friend of B.F. Skinner. Her mother volunteered building houses. My new roommate, she was red-haired and freckled and pure Ralph Lauren.

I'd had a paper route. I worked as a telemarketer. I served Dog-on-a-Stick in the mall for three months. I'd never seen a polo pony in my life.

Our room was a narrow tunnel with two beds opposite each other and fastened to the walls. We had two corkboards, one over each bed, also attached to the wall, and nothing on the corkboards so far. There were two dressers, one to either side of the door, a mirror over each dresser and a single window at the far end with the wide window ledge adopted now as Kyra's throne. The room was completely symmetrical, as though planned for identical twins.

A picture of Kyra with a famous football player, taken on a nude beach and torn from a Spanish newspaper, fell from a notebook as she took up her unpacking. She reached for the picture and stuck the picture to her mirror with chewing gum.

She said, "I freebased with an old man at the airport coming up here. Can you believe it? This old dude."

I barely knew what she meant. I came to school on the Greyhound, with a hamburger in a paper bag and a mystery novel to read on the way. I was polite when a man my father's age asked me questions. Now I threw myself across my bed, and shook the hair out of my eyes. Under my hand, my new comforter was so cheap and thin it was a prop more than a quilt. It was a fake pattern of homey comfort, polyester squares over polyester fill. I said, "What's up for tonight?"

Night, in the dorms, was the worst sort of deal. It was crucial to not be at home, in our room, alone. It was too obvious if you didn't have someplace to go. To make friends, you have to have friends. It's like making sourdough bread from sourdough starter.

Kyra looked at me without answering. Assessing. Then she said, "Don't be such a kitten." She leaned forward and snorted another line. She wiped her nose with the back of her hand, and pushed the mirror toward me.

Craig was tall. That's something I like. He had wide shoulders and was a swimmer. He was in somebody's room, I don't know whose, where they were mixing Margaritas. By the time Kyra and I got there, still early in the night, they'd run out of ice. Craig picked up a mustard yellow plastic pitcher stolen from Student Services. He said, "No worries."

I liked the sound of that—no worries. I was all worries. No worries was about the cushion of money: Cocaine and Margaritas. Nude beaches. Freebasing.

Craig's plan was to break into the closed cafeteria. An ice machine in the cafeteria spit a constant bin of cubes. Kyra put a finger to my ribs and mouthed the words, "Go with him."

I whispered, "What if he gets caught? I'd get kicked out of school." From below the cocaine, the worries surfaced. They eased their way into mind: school, money, grades, sex.

"You're ten thousand in debt, and it's only the first week. Think they'll kick you out for stealing ice?" she said. "Go. He likes you." The virginity thing. She poked me in the ribs again, with one sharp finger.

Craig was a swimmer, that's all I knew. We went down the dorm's narrow hall and then down three short stairs. I said, "What do you swim?" Outside, our forest of a campus was barely lit by glowing orbs, the air damp in gleaming halos around faint lights. We stepped into the night onto the lush, dark grounds.

He said, "Relay, mostly. Sometimes dive."

I said, "I run the eight hundred, in the spring."

"Eight-eighty?" he said. Same race, different measurement. I'd remember his way for next time.

The ground was a rough mix of slopes and sinkholes you wouldn't know were there to look. The silhouette of a person marked the distance at times. Mostly, the campus was empty, lights on in dorms, music floating from parties. We cut cross country, ignored the trail, and walked in wet grass. I walked barefoot. My shoes, cheap sandals, were back in the party room. I tried not to worry about my shoes. A light rain fell like glitter.

I wrapped my arm through Craig's. He looked surprised—a nervousness around his mouth, eyes on me—but didn't pull his arm away. The heat of his arm was like a fireplace, a ski lodge. He was the heated leather seat of a good Mercedes. In the house I'd come from, where I grew up, we didn't even have this much heat in the furnace.

The Student Center was flat and low, a three-story building built into the side of a hill. The Student Center looked like it was sinking, the way the building fell into the earth.

My favorite building was the Dean's House. The Dean's House was brick and older, the original homestead of the millionaire who founded the place—the millionaire who set up a school for the children of millionaires, and for a few scholarship kids like me. The Dean's House was almost a church; it didn't sink into the earth, but thrust itself up, communing only with the sky, like it barely needed the support of our planet at all. The Student Center was the opposite: squat and functional, subservient to student needs, housing Student Services.

It was the weight of student needs, it seemed, that ran the building into the ground, and pushed it deep into the side of the sloping hill, like an old woman with hunched shoulders.

Craig and I were one more demand on the old woman that was Student Services, now.

We walked in and made it as far as the mailboxes, but couldn't get to the cafeteria with the ice machine. The doors to the cafeteria were locked, a heavy link of chain wrapped through the door handles. There were people still in the back of the cafeteria. Laborers. I heard their voices in fast, slangy Spanish, a radio on, the spray of water and clang of metal pans hitting together.

Behind those chained doors, it was like the workers never went home. They were locked in and part of Student Services, like the ice, supplied to meet our needs. I'd been a dishwasher once in high school. Now I was one small step over, on the party side of that dividing line. One step made all the difference.

We walked around the building in search of a back door, and found a row of narrow windows open to let the heat out from the dishwashers' work. Industrial equipment beat a rhythm inside. A conveyor belt carried dishes and trays through steam for sterilization. The windows we needed were on the first floor and open, but the ground sloped down and made the windows beyond easy reach.

I said, "Give me a step. I'll get in." I'd earn my way. I brushed off one damp and dirty bare foot. My skirt was short and full, cheap summer cotton bought with Dog-On-A-Stick money.

Craig folded his fingers together. I stepped on his hand. His hand was warm under my cold instep. I got a hold of the window. He kept one hand under my foot and put the other on my shin. He lifted me. We were acrobats. I stepped on his shoulder, and on his arched back, where I felt his bones and muscle under my toes. I'd jumped harder hurdles than an open window enough times before, with less incentive even. I'd chaffed my legs on canvas hurdles meant for quick release at track. I'd tripped in high jump and once broke an ankle in a cemetery. That's what high school was about—training in track, in volleyball and cross-country. High school was training for late night drinking in off-limits alleys, knowing how to run fast. High school was prep for college.

The window I climbed through now was simple, hidden in the center of the lush fields of our private school, under a dark sky and far from city lights, far from cops or neighbors beyond the dorm kids. Every star overhead was an accomplice, paid for by the winking rich. And I joined the privileged ranks as I slipped through the half-open window, scraping my thigh on the aluminum of the window frame. I stepped a bare foot onto the newly mopped gleam of our dining hall. My foot left a dirty print, the shape of my toes on the floor. It didn't matter. Everything was meant for us. We were the clients, the customers. I heard the rush and clang of dishwashers around the corner, loading our dishes into industrial machines.

I walked alongside the steel tables, behind the giant walk-in, and out into the cafeteria. The dishwashers had their radio on loud. I plunged the plastic pitcher into a mountain of ice. Ice in abundance, waiting for me. There was so much ice piled in the metal bin, it had its own fog bank like a miniature mountain.

I started to climb back out the window with the plastic pitcher in my teeth. Then I gagged. I stopped. Below me was lit only where the half-light of indoors seeped out. Craig was illuminated in pieces: curly hair, a sculpted shoulder, pale feet severed by the lines of Birkenstocks. His hands reached up, glowing in the florescent light. I dropped the pitcher straight down.

Craig caught the pitcher easily. Ice bounced out the top. Together, we exercised the beauty of team sports, well trained. Craig put the pitcher on the ground. He made himself into a ladder; I stepped down into the near dark, and trusted in the strength of his shoulders. Trusted Craig's body.

"Chinese acrobats," he said. "You're good."

I slid down, until my thighs were around his neck. He put his hands on my thighs. I ran a hand through his hair, my skirt bunched up high along his shoulders. He wobbled as he bent to pick up the pitcher, still holding me on his back. A kinetic human sculpture. I rode him like an elephant. I giggled. "You're strong."

"A swimmer," he said, reminding me again. "That's what we're good for."

I slid down his back, easing my legs over his muscles, feet to the ground. We headed toward the dorm, the party, and I wrapped my arm through his. Muscle to muscle, his biceps and mine. I felt like a horse, an animal, roaming a field, a scratch on my thigh. I could climb anything. Craig looked down at me, his face close to mine but above. He said, "I have rum in my room."

I said, "I do, too. And whiskey." It wasn't my whiskey but Kyra's. She said rum was for high school, for pouring into soda and sneaking into hockey games when you're hoping for a fight. Rum was to whiskey what speed was to cocaine, meaning last year and not good enough now.

These were the rules I learned, the beginning of school. Rules brought from Andover and Exeter, Choate, Hill and beyond.

We reached Craig's dorm first. In Craig's building, the beds were set up with one across the far end of the room and a second alongside near the door. "Which one's yours?"

He pointed, and I sat down. There was no place else to sit besides on one bed or the other. In our room, Kyra and I would sit on the tall, built-in dressers, leaning against the mirrors with our feet dangling. Craig pulled a bottle of Bacardi from his closet and put ice in a plastic cup. "That's all I've got." No mixer.

I didn't care about the rum. I could've used another line of coke, to start the buzz all over again, to keep my confidence up. I put my glass on the floor and pulled Craig by one arm. I said, "Did that hurt your shoulder, when I stood on it?"

Wouldn't want to fuck up his relay. I put my hand where earlier I'd had my foot. I put a second hand on the round ring of chew that wore through his jeans where a wallet could've been. Craig's breath was sharp with alcohol, lips chapped.

He found a condom in a drawer. I was glad about the condom, since I hadn't thought of that part. I was only thinking how ready I was to move past the virgin stage, to not have to worry again about accidentally telling people what I hadn't already done.

Craig was an acre of chlorine and sun-polished skin. A smooth back, muscles like continents defining the geography. His thighs were hard, his cock hard. I felt him push himself into me, and I let it happen like I was watching from a faraway place.

This is how it works: skin to skin, muscle to muscle, bodies moving. Outside to inside. I wasn't wet—it was all too fast—and the rubber caught on the folds of my skin. I said, "Shit," and flinched.

He ducked back, the muscles of his butt taut under my hands. "Shh, shhh" he said. He dug in the drawer for a bottle of lube. And then Craig's thighs were pushing against my thighs. His swimmer's back was under my hands, my skirt up, my clothes mostly still on. He pushed himself inside of me. I could hardly feel my own body, could feel only pressure, and sweat on my skin. When it was over, I saw blood on the condom he threw in the trash. There was a small patch of blood the shape of Africa on his sheets.

One hurdle over, the goal met.

Craig's crowded room smelled like bong water and dirty laundry. There was sand in his bed. I climbed over him, put my underwear back on. "I need to find Kyra. She'll be looking for me."

Kyra and I might snort another line. I picked up the pitcher full of ice. None of the ice had even pretended to melt, that's how fast the sex had been. It made me sad, for a minute; I guess in part I'd hoped that somehow the sex had taken longer, and it only seemed like time moved quickly. Instead, climbing out the window onto Craig's back had been more substantial, more exciting. Now I waited with one hand on the door handle while he pulled on his jeans, tucked in his t-shirt and slipped his feet in the Birkenstocks.

Back at the party room dorm, the party was huge. The crowd had overflowed the room, spread to the lounge. I knew almost nobody. They'd been making drinks without the ice, the idea of Margaritas long forgotten. The music was loud and the lights were off and everybody had cigarettes glowing orange around the room. Craig walked ahead of me. Somebody said, "My man!" and slapped Craig on the back. I walked the other way, cutting through the crowd—I didn't need to hold his hand all night.

I was one of them now. I didn't know them, but I was one. Experienced, indulged. A thief, and not a virgin either. I saw a freshman I'd met before, a guy named Dave. "Where's Kyra?"

He shrugged, raising his shoulders. He yelled back, over the music, "Haven't seen her."

Out a narrow window I saw the glow of more cigarettes, a cluster of people, and the white flame of one candle burning. A second arm of the party, outdoors.

I went out. Kyra was there, cross-legged, balanced on a cement retaining wall. There were other people I didn't know sitting on the wall and on a blanket in the damp grass, drinking wine from a bottle. Kyra's eyes were half closed and cat-angled.

She said, "So... score?"

I didn't say anything, only laughed and looked away.

She said, "Hey, how was it?"

The wine-drinkers looked at me, too. I ignored them, sat close to Kyra on the wall. I said as quietly as seemed reasonable, talking to her alone, "Nothing to write home about." I could still feel the ghost of Craig's weight against mine. I needed a shower. I looked at my leg below my shorts, thinking there might be blood or spew or sweat dripping, but there was only the red line of a scratch from the window I hurdled.

Kyra laughed. "Doesn't have to be anything the first time." She said, "Let's get out of here. Let's get a cab and go downtown, see this city."

Leave the paradise of our campus? The night was soft and damp. I didn't want to leave.

I said, "I left my shoes inside." We could see the party through the window, hear the music and voices loud in the air.

The front lobby of the dorm had lights that never turned off. Security lights, glaring and bright. The rooms off to the sides were pitch dark. In the middle of the overly lit hallway, a group of five guys stood in a half-circle outside the dorm's dark lounge. I recognized two of them: a swimmer and a lacrosse guy. Not the others. One sat on the floor, his head in his hands.

We walked up. The standing guys stepped toward us, the half circle closing in.

One said, "We'd like to know where you've been." I'd never seen him before, far as I could remember. Curly hair, skinny.

Kyra, at my elbow, laughed. "Go ahead, tell 'em where you've been, kitten."

I said, "Fuck that." It was my business. I still had to think about where I'd been. I'd save the thinking part for later, for being sober and back on the ground again.

Another guy said, "There's weed missing."

Kyra said, "You probably smoked it and forgot."

"We noticed you've been coming and going, disappearing somewhere. We thought maybe you had it." It was the curly haired guy again.

I was two steps behind, and not paying the right kind of attention. I said, "There's got to be enough pot on this campus for everybody." There were drugs in every room. Psychedelics grew on the football field. Pot came with the terrain; I saw it as part of my scholarship.

Another one said, "Not our pot, and not for you. And it was a fair amount."

Kyra was a corporate lawyer's daughter. She said, "You better justify your accusations before you go throwing words around." She could talk law even through the drugs, through the drink.

The guy on the floor was pink skinned with thin hair the color of weak beer. He lifted his head from his hands. He said, "Fuck you, bitch."

That's all it took. Kyra was a whirlwind of polo pony muscle, a hard punch thrown square, fighting in a way I'd never seen a woman fight. It was the same way she cut lines, fast and sure. I stepped back. I said, "Jesus!"

This was muscles put to use. All the indulgence, the training, the coke. The flat belly. My muscles came from step aerobics, from track and field, volleyball.

Kyra was coming on fast. The guy on the floor couldn't get up. He couldn't crabwalk away. Either he or Kyra kicked a plastic cup and beer splattered over the wall, the cup rattling loud. A passing drunk raised his glass and said, "Ho ho!" as though this were something to see. Another jumped in. He grabbed Kyra, ducked her fists and elbows, and tried to pull her away.

I watched like I was watching TV. Then I said, "Kyra, let's go. Forget it." I stepped in, too. I reached low, and tried to pry the matted tangle of Kyra and the frat boys apart. Everything smelled like smoke and whiskey and cologne, hair gel and herbal deodorant. Kyra didn't seem to hear me. She swung blind until more than one of us was able to lock our arms around her and pull her off. Then the guys let go but I held on, my arms around her shoulders. I steered her out, and didn't care about getting my shoes anymore. They were only old and worn sandals anyway, part of my past more than the future.

Kyra let me pull her out. She half-turned in my arms and yelled back over my shoulder, "You better think who you're calling 'bitch.' You better be on your feet next time, motherfucker."

She could've gotten away from me if she wanted to, pushed me aside and gone back to the fight. Instead she quit struggling. She walked alongside me. She said, "He wouldn't talk to a man that way. He wouldn't sit on the floor and make accusations. I had to wake him up."

I said, "Well, you did that."

A goose-egg on her cheekbone had started to swell. The bump of the goose-egg only set off her narrow nose, her Spanish-beach freckles. It made me wish for a goose-egg on my cheek, too. She was a cover girl for a boxing magazine now, a prize fighter. A goose-egg model. Her eyes were closer to closed than ever. When I let go of her shoulders, she stayed by my side and quit clenching and unclenching her fists, instead linked her arm in mine, holding my hand, acting like the hand holding was normal. She made me nervous. My feet were cold and sore, still bare, my thighs sweaty. I heard the voices from the party like one solid sound, like music.

I looked back, and saw Craig through the window. He was in the lit space of a side room. He used his swimmer's muscles, his wide shoulders, to heft a pony keg high over the heads of fellow frat boys. His face was flushed. He looked warm and sweet and stoned, embedded in the party we'd never be asked back to.

My heater. King of the condom, the sheet stained like Africa.

I stood in the dark outside the party, looking in.

Kyra said, "So, what else is up? Still want to head downtown?" It was late, almost time for clubs to close. I knew downtown. Downtown was where I'd come from, before the scholarship, before school. The grid of bus malls and clubs. She put a hand to her bruised face. "Got that ice?" She looked right at me and she laughed. Her model laugh, her perfect teeth. Her complete confidence.

And I lived where she lived now. Our matching beds, our symmetrical space. I'd been assigned as her roommate, as though given a scholarship to the life.

It didn't matter where we went next. Kyra's invitation was what mattered. To make friends, you have to have friends. Kyra would bring me along into her world of polo playing and coke, nude beaches and pro football players. I'd passed some kind of test, and it was all a test, an ongoing parade. This was our gymkhana: drugs, sex, and fighting. Agility trials. It was a polo pony show; Kyra would be my trainer.

Then I was nervous, but in a good way—nerves making my step light and stomach floaty. I said, "Sure, downtown. Let's go."

I had to look away when I said it, to the dark of the sprawling lawn. I didn't want Kyra to recognize so quickly what I was just starting to learn: she was the kind of animal I'd follow anywhere.

## Night Trilogy

Aimee Bender

### I. Broke

He met a woman with eyes so black they woke up the nocturnal mammals. If you looked close enough—if she let you—if you were her lover and lucky enough to see in that intently—you could, on a summer night, find Orion near her left pupil. The great hunter. Watch out. Those seven little dots glittering, scattered on the iris, were like brands of longing on the heart of the looker, and she never left a man complete. For the rest of their lives, memories of the slippery line of her back would flit into their minds, while driving through traffic, while frying bacon, while washing sand from their child's hands after a long reddening day at the beach. Look into the sky on a dark summer night, and there, huge, is the eye of the woman you once loved like a rocket. Try to survive that.

II. WINTER

Oh PLEASE. Says the man to the woman. Oh PLEASE.

WHAT? she replies.

He stirs his melted ice cream with a metal spoon. The waiter returns with the card printout and a pen from another restaurant and gives the check to the wrong person.

Thank you, says the waiter to their profiles.

WHAT?

Someone removes the melted ice cream bowl. There are little droplets congealing on the placemat, white-yellow.

Add a tip. Sign the name. Flourish. Take the yellow slip and leave the white one. Put it in the coat pocket. Get up. Locate the rest of the coat under the seat; slide it on. Button all four buttons. Flip the collar.

Thank you, says the maitre d' before the door that leads outside.

The man: straight ahead, no response. The woman: nods. Rolls a toothpick out of the turning plastic toothpick holder.

On the street the air is fifty knives of cold. This is not Alaska.

Why did we move here? I thought it would be warmer here, one of them thinks. The weather reports say records are breaking, daily; usually it's balmy this time of year. Some of the kids are building sleds, hopeful.

Her collar up around her ears. His hands deep in his pockets. She is walking slower, toothpicking, and finally stops. He keeps going, swift.

Each of his lower teeth is nestled in line with its upper neighbor.

She sees a window full of coats. For every season. She is all coat right now. Fake fur collar and deep wool pockets. Inside her pockets, you can find lipstick, some tissue, a restaurant yellow slip, and several candy wrappers. Soon, a used toothpick. Inside the coats in the window, all the pockets are empty. She is dreaming into them. How good it would be to have a coat with empty pockets. You could spend a whole lifetime and put nothing in them, ever, and die with enough space to fill a thousand cold hands.

III. NIGHT

She does everything she can to avoid it. She goes to sleep right when the sun sinks. She rises when it rises. That's too much sleep but she keeps herself sleeping, keeps herself under pillows, and all day has something of that achey over-drowsy feeling she remembers from days as a child when she had the flu, the endless flu when everyone else was in school. She does not want to see the night anymore. She wants to see all things at once, the world drenched in yellow sunlight, people up, horns honking, alert teeth, caffeine and the knowable.

The birds call to her, those birds who are awake when it's dark out. Get up, they call, when she's slept out her exhaustion. Get up, come out here, come out up into the trees.

She soaks bird seed in poison and places it on her windowsill in an attractive basket, but they have fine senses of smell and only the moths and mosquitoes make the mistake.

On the one day, they get her up. They're so loud, cackling and flirting in the bushy trees, and she has slept and slept and it's only four in the morning. That's what happens when you go to bed at six-thirty.

She steps out the screen door and the sidewalk is covered in bird shit. The birds slip out of the tree like maidens undressing and land, delicately, upon her. Shoo, she says, with no emphasis at all. All the windows are dark. All the cars are parked. Everyone in the world is unconscious. She has taken sleeping pills and drank four glasses of warm milk but you cannot defeat your own wakefulness. The sitting up of her heart; the trainwreck of her mind. She is not crying, not yet. She is covered in birds like a coat rack, preening and cooing, and each bird is waiting for the tears as their cue, before they will spring off of her all at once, in a shadowy coat, and begin their migration to the ocean.

## Pre-Supper Clubbing

### Jeff Johnson

Her dad stood in the backyard, poking at a wounded cardinal with a stick that had fallen off of a diseased elm. At dusk it still had to be at least ninety degrees out. Even the grass looked hot.

The dad wore long pants the color of butter brickle ice cream and an undershirt. V-neck. We were getting ready for one of those summer dinners. You go into a steakhouse with some old people at 5:30, and they're done and in bed by 9:00. You just mind your manners.

The bird was one of those things that couldn't wait for some reason. Something that gums everything up, like having to move a hide-a-bed into a dorm while somewhere else a keg of expensive beer is being drained by everyone you know.

The dad prodded the cardinal like a cooking turkey. Nothing was happening, except the bird was sinking in on itself like an old pie. The dad shook his head, not saying much, just shrugging and mumbling about the bird's misery. He summoned for her mom to get a blanket or a towel.

"I'm not using the good towels," she said. Made it clear.

"Did I say good towels?" he asked. "Specifically?" he asked. He didn't wait for her to keep complaining. "Cardinals are rare now," he said.

I sat on the wicker chaise with an iced tea. Stayed put. I was a guest. It was their lawn. Their stick. Their towels. Their daughter. Besides, I was already in my dinner suit.

The dad went to put on a pair of golf gloves, muttering should he just kill it. Is it sickly or something?

He returned from the garage and proceeded to jab at it more with the stick.

"I'm trying to find out where it hurts," he said. "Aww, jeez," he winced as the bird made an attempt to flap away, or just to please wave the dad off. Let it die alone.

"That ain't going anywhere." The dad shook his head. The stick snapped in two. Bark splintered and flaked around the bird.

Now her uncle, who'd been napping, stuck his head out the back screen, ignoring me. He pushed the door open into the chaise with his gut and see-sawed floss through his teeth. He'd just finished up a four or five-hour shower and had been sequestered in front of the "good mirror" bare naked, checking his teeth, cuddling his privates like they were the special pork chops for the Queen.

"Bird?" he asked.

"Cardinal," the dad replied, and raised a hand like he had the situation covered.

"What do you know about birds?" the uncle scoffed.

"You've never tended to an animal," the dad said, "not once," and looked at the girl. "Can't you find me a new stick?" he asked her.

"Getting to be supper time," the uncle changed the subject. Before anyone answered, he asked the dad, "Golf gloves?"

The dad waved him off. "I hate to kill such a creature," he said.

"You aren't killing anything," the mom said.

"Just look at it though," the dad said. "In our yard like this. I'm just afraid that tabby might get it." He pointed over the back fence to a neighbor's lawn.

"That tabby's on a goddamn string," the mom said.

"Canned beer?" the uncle asked.

The dad waved him off again and just said, "Full fridge."

"Before dinner?" the uncle asked.

"Yeah, yeah, knock yourself out," the dad said.

The bird was coated in what looked like a runny yolk now. Oozed. The girl threw up in the bushes. Chex mix. Then dry heaved. "Cut the drama," the mom said.

"Bird make her sick?" the uncle questioned, then air-elbowed me.

"Spoiled cheese," I lied.

"Hon, get me one of those garden rocks," the dad said. "Hon?"

"You sure?" the mom asked and picked one up. A maroon one. Volcanic. Lighter than it looked.

The dad put the old towel over the cardinal. A fly snapped into a blue zapper in the neighboring yard. "Zzzip," said the uncle. Grill smells were wafting our way. Reminding us we were putting off dinner.

The dad threw the rock down hard on the towel and missed a little. The bird let out a faint squawk and wobbled out from under the towel.

"Try again," the uncle asked. "Looks like he..."

"He look dead to you, Paul?" the dad interrupted the uncle. Disgusted.

"S'pose not," the uncle said about five minutes later. The bird lolled around on its back. Beak wide open. Eyes gray.

The dad closed his eyes and kicked the bird back under the towel. Soccer style. Sweat beaded up on his forehead. He looked like he was getting audited. "Get me my golf cleats," he said to the girl.

The dad sat on the deck and laced the shoes. The uncle emitted a slight belch and measured his nose hairs with his upper lip.

With his golf cleats on, he went back to the shivering lump under the towel. Everyone was mad now. Starving.

"How's your ice tea, your majesty?" the mom said to me. I hadn't moved from the chaise, except to fetch the newspaper from the front porch.

"Cubed sugar?" the uncle asked me. He squeezed his index finger and thumb together in a cube-sized motion.

"No, thank you," I said.

"Visiting the girl?" the uncle asked. I waved him off and read the classifieds. Checked the movies.

The mom huffed inside to watch a videotape. *The Fantastiks.* Chilled Chardonnay.

The girl sat in the garage on an old raft. Spun the wheels on some skates.

Now the dad reset the towel. Stomped, or stamped, if you will. Pretty soon holes were torn in the old towel and nothing moved underneath it anymore.

## Suite 1306

### James Tate

Ginger had agreed to have a drink with that hairy, fat sales rep from Parkers, Herb what's-his-name, first, because she had already refused him on at least five previous occasions, and she couldn't risk losing the account—he was that type, he would take his business elsewhere—and, well, Michael had called and cancelled their date to go dancing, he was going to his mother's, birthday, something, she hadn't really listened to his explanation after first catching the drift. Michael was not to be counted on these days, she seemed to be last on his list of priorities ever since she had declined his marriage proposal. She didn't want to marry, once was enough, thank you. She wanted to have a good time.

Staying at the Plaza was fun. She mingled easily with the glamorous people in the lobby, French businessmen, heiresses from Palm Beach and Newport, movie stars—Jean Paul Belmondo had tried out his line on her last year, "Have pity on an old man, my child. Let us compromise our lives wantonly!"—and famous writers. Yes, she was a presence in the Oak Room and the Russian Tea Room.

Whether or not management and the bartenders knew it, high-priced hookers worked the room with a panther's grace. Ginger adored this part of her cocktail hour after the day's work. She knew their moves, how they followed men out of the room on their way to the restroom downstairs. She knew what the women looked for: out-of-towners, a little tight, with money, vulnerable and randy. Most of the hookers that could make it in The Plaza were extremely beautiful and well-dressed. They could approach a single or a pair of gentlemen without attracting the least bit of attention. And what man, in the city without his wife, would complain to the management that a beautiful woman wanted to share a drink with him? Ginger had never seen one turned away, at least not for a drink. These women fascinated her. She had always meant to strike up a conversation with one.

As she dressed for her drink with hairy Herb she sipped from a glass of wine, washed down a little speed and puffed on a joint of some California sinsemilla her friend Laurie had sent her last week. I mean, she certainly intended to be a little buzzed to get through with this sleaze-bag. Maybe it could even be fun. Why not? Give the guy a bone and leave him sweating. The bar was crowded and she stood there at the entrance surveying the scene.

From behind her hands were placed lightly above her hips. "My, aren't we looking sexy," he whispered into her ear.

"Nice line, Herb. Cut the shit and find us a table."

Drinks were ordered, a Margarita for Ginger and a bourbon and water for Herb.

"You know, Ginger, you were magnificent today, a real ballbuster. You made Larry squirm, that's an achievement."

"Larry's a pussy-whipped wimp, just like you, Herb. He gave me what I wanted because I let him get a peek up my shirt. Saved me major bucks and he went home happy."

"If it's money you're interested in, sweetie, I could get into that."

Ginger smiled, her cruelest, sexiest, as though that were not out of the realm of possibility. Herb sipped at his drink through a straw and looked up at her. She was looking mean tonight, flecked blond hair, green eyes lit with mischief. Proud and desperate to be whatever it was she was.

"Ginger, I know you think I'm some kind of ... greaseball ... salesman, but I've got a heart, too, and I, well, I think you're one of the most attractive women I've ever met." Herb sported muttonchops and a plaid wool tie; he was married to someone even more overweight than himself, and there was little love lost between them.

"I don't think you're a greaseball, Herb. You just leer a lot. You know what I mean by 'leer,' Herb? A woman knows what's on your mind. When we're supposed to be talking prices, you're actually thinking 'pussy,' you're thinking 'tits,' you're thinking you'd like nothing better than to stick your dick in my mouth. A woman knows these things, Herb. You're not as subtle as you'd like to think."

Herb was blushing now, speechless to hear Ginger use words like that. It excited him terribly, but it was also embarrassing. Hookers talked like that. He paid them to talk that way, but not attractive, respectable businesswomen, at least not in his experience.

"Well, it is true that I've had fantasies about you..." He sipped at his drink, unable to meet her sadistic gaze. Why had it started out like this? This wasn't how he had imagined their "date." He wanted to impress her with his considerate, tender, curious, witty charms. He knew she thought him to be coarse, coarser than the fashionable, younger people he imagined her dancing with after meetings when she came to town.

"Let's hear them, tell me your fantasies about me." Ginger's head was fairly spinning with the mixture of tequila and speed and sinsemilla. She was having a surprisingly good time making Herb squirm. She ordered another round from the waitress.

"No, Ginger, let's talk about something else. I didn't mean for it to be like this, honestly. I wanted you to... like me. I wanted to make you laugh."

"But I am laughing, Herb. You said you'd had fantasies about me. I'm just curious. Was I good? Did you do anything weird to me, Herb? Because I'm not into being tied up or, you know, whips or anything."

"There was nothing like that, Ginger, I promise you. It's just that... No, I can't say it. Tell me about your house in Connecticut." He was sweating now. Herb always sweated. His chin was permanently pressed against his chest now. He made eye contact with Ginger only furtively now and then, knowing that she was mocking him.

"Herb, you're being an ass now. Come on, I want to hear what you do to me in your dreams. Anything involving chocolate or electric appliances? Tell me, I'm flattered. You'll cheer me up if you tell me. Otherwise, this is going to be a dull evening, okay?"

"It's nothing special, Ginger."

"Nothing special? Well, thanks a lot! That takes the cake!"

"No, I didn't mean it like that. You know what I mean. I mean, we just do it, very romantically, very slowly, tenderly, and it's... it's beautiful and..."

"And what, Herb? And what?"

"And well, you know."

"No, I don't know, Herb. It's your fantasy, I don't know."

"And you tell me I'm the best you've ever had. That's all."

Ginger couldn't restrain herself now and burst out laughing. Of all the fantasies he might have confessed, this one struck her as the funniest. "You're really something else, Herb. You know that?"

"I'm sorry, Ginger. Really I am. Forgive me." He reached across the table tentatively and took her hand in his. He knew his was damp and he wasn't entirely in control. Ginger was repulsed at first, but then realized what she had done. She had lured him into her trap, and had forced him into it, and then mocked him savagely.

"It was a sweet fantasy, Herb. I don't know what made me laugh, I'm sorry."

They sat there in silence holding hands across the table. Ginger had spent her venom for the moment. Herb's confidence was slowly coming back to him. He even allowed himself to think: I've got her where I want her now.

"So what do you think, baby, shall we have one more round? You're already home, just take the elevator to bed. How's your room, by the way? Got a view this time?"

Ginger withdrew her hand slowly and finished her drink. "Sure, why not? Let's have another. The room's great, you know, magic fingers and soft porn on the cable. I could live in this hotel. Great room service, all these sexy Italian bellhops."

"You're too much, Ginger, you know that? If you were mine I'd give you anything in the world. Honest, I would. Nothing would be too much for you."

Ginger smiled. "How much for one night?" she said. She hadn't really meant to say it, it just leapt out automatically under her breath.

"What did you say?"

"I said, how much for one night? How much would you pay to, uh, have your way with me?"

Herb sat up straight now, the first time since sitting down. He looked her straight in the eyes. Was she starting up the game again? Was she mocking?

"You're not serious."

"Oh, I'm serious, Herb. I want to know, how much for one evening, straight, nothing weird, how much would you pay me?"

He was scratching his head and pulling at his muttonchops. "I don't know, I'd have to think about it. You're not serious?"

"Herb, you said if I was yours nothing would be too much. So I just want to know how much it would be worth to you to have me for one night."

"Maybe three hundred. How does three hundred sound? That's more than these girls get," he looked around the room and, sure enough, there were at least three girls working the room right then.

"Yeah, but I'm not a hooker, Herb. I'm me, your fantasy girl. You know I'd never fuck you without some special incentive. Three hundred's chicken feed. I wouldn't let you squeeze my left tit for three hundred."

Herb was puzzled now. Every time he made an effort to get the conversation on to something other than sex, this incredibly beautiful, younger businesswoman worked it back to dirty talk.

"How much?" she repeated. "How much would you pay, Herb?"

"Well, I'm maybe not as rich as I let on. I don't know, I guess I could come up with five, six hundred."

"For six hundred I'll dance naked for you but no touching, nothing." Jesus Christ, Herb thought to himself, this woman is serious. She must be loaded. And then he thought, why not? Go for it. Fuck this dame, just plain fuck this beautiful dame because I am never going to have another chance.

"A thousand," he said. "A thousand for the night, and that's my last offer."

"Let's go," she said.

If rooms could talk, if Suite 1306 could tell its long, jagged story. At eight o'clock on this particular Monday evening, a shapely blond woman with green eyes undressed before a perspiring middle-aged overweight man. Neither spoke. The caustic jibes had ceased in the elevator. Now Ginger's hands shook as she removed each article of clothing. Herb sat on the edge of the bed tapping the fingers of his hands together. Then she tossed her sheer bikini panties over her shoulder and said, "There." It was all done. She had had her appendix removed, he noticed that first.

Herb was a gentle lover. He never took his eyes off hers for the four hours they were in bed together. And he spoke only to ask if this was good, if this pleased her. And she said yes, yes, as if in a dream.

Michael called from the lobby around nine the next morning. In her room they shared a breakfast of cafe au lait and croissants with butter and jam. It really had been his mother's birthday and he was sorry to have cancelled their plans. She told him she had stayed in and watched a movie on TV. She was hoping he would ask her to marry him again. She even thought of telling him that a man had offered her a thousand dollars for one night. Think of the money that he, Michael, would be saving in a lifetime of thousand-dollar nights. Suddenly, with no warning, she started to cry.

## It's Not Black; It's Always Darker Than That

**Lucy Thomas**

I know the colors at night; they speak in gutteral voices. Things were never the way Edward claimed and now we all know why.

In the one night you asked about, I was hiding by the shed, ready to kick a snake if a snake oozed over my foot. Snakes and similar animals fly differently than inanimate objects, when sent airborne, and this is why we hate to see living things thrown or dropped.

Edward was with the neighbor-woman, the one who does her laundry in that room under her house. He had gone over to tell her he'd be using the chainsaw in the morning; he didn't want her to wake up. But he'd been gone for forty minutes, so I was out by the shed, with a view through her back window, seeing if through the night I could find them betraying me.

The night was liquid. This was Maryland in July, not far from the water, where the jellyfish were everywhere. The air gave us no answers at all—it lulled me into a trance of some kind. A trance that made me want something terrible to happen. If not the betrayal by my husband, something more violent and irreparable.

But I would not create this. I would only watch. There are times, maybe four times a day, when you are constitutionally ready to see something horrific. At night this rate is higher.

## What We Do Is Secret

### Thorn Kief Hillsbery

FLAVOR CHECK, LEXINGTON AND MANSFIELD, 11 P.M.
BLACK CHERRY.

It's not what you'd call my pick to lick, it reminds me of a Robo high, and I'm definitely over my thirst for the worst. Robitussin's evil shit, man. Like your head's wrapped in layers of those stringy flat bandages, or maybe it's Kotex, layers of creepy clinging Kotex that itch and smother you all at once. You get fuzzy sloppy too with Quaaludes, but at least you laugh, you can be falling down a flight of stairs on 'ludes and laughing like the audience on *I Love Lucy*. On Robo you're nothing but a sick fuck zombie. But back in the day, when the Punk Crash Pad was at the Hollywood Towers, lots of times that's all we had. We'd lift it from Ralph's on Sunset late at night, I had Health and Beauty memorized down to the eyebrow tweezers, we'd jam down the aisle with our hair under caps for urban camo and just snag it on the move, not even stopping, off their shelf and down your shorts, the first thing you do on a Robo run is grab your tighty-whities.

And there was one checker there who must have been a nympho, she played watch the crotch like some good citizens play the slots in Vegas, but obviously not for security purposes since she never busted us, and we made it part of our regularly scheduled programming to go to her lane with our diversionary Big Hunks in hand after Donny Rose let it slip to her accidentally on purpose once upon a time that he had the biggest package in the whole scene, which he actually supposedly did even though he just turned twelve. And from then on he always joked about introducing her to Big Jim and the Twins, and gave a little squeeze to the Robo through his jeans.

Then we'd bail for home street home. The juice was cut completely at the Towers and none of us could A the Q how to run the elevators off D-size Duracells, so we just climbed the fire stairs five summer stories or so, past where any of the street trash squatters ever had the guts or glory for, and just for insurance against any dirtbags, scumbags, or elderqueers who maybe did, we built some booby traps, like, for example you counted six steps above the sixth floor landing and then six more which added up to 666, the Sign of the Beast, so you remembered where the big Mazola slick was that we poured on the stairs that otherwise you'd slip on in the dark and reach for the handrail which we studded with about a hundred single-edge razor blades stuck in blobs of Bazooka bubblegum. And likewise we did a sharpened bamboo pungee stick thing with rat poison on the tips nine steps times two above the ninth floor landing in honor of that English band, 999.

The bad planning part of this was that coming down there weren't any handy-dandy memory aids like six-six-six or nine-nine-nine, since twelve steps above the sixth floor turns out to be seven steps below the seventh floor or some shit like that, and it's just too many numbers to keep straight in your head period, let alone comma, and here the comma comes before especially when you're loaded on cough syrup and you're ten years old. Because Donny was the oldest one of all of us and he was older by a year at least. I mean my day job for a while there was laying on the roof of the Towers with my shirt off and my hands behind my head, not to get a tan but hoping Our Mister Sun might sprout some foliage in my armpits.

Now I stick to night work only. I tell everyone I'm the watchman at the Jell-O factory same way's Rodney Bingenheimer's the mayor of Sunset Strip, unofficially and pointlessly, but still it means something, it means there's someone after dark who cares at least that Jell-O was actually invented, lots of people with advanced degrees don't know that, and not in some laboratory back East, either, but right here in Hollywood, around the corner from Cinema Research, one block north of Santa Monica, there's a plaque and everything.

And too it means there's someone keeping track of the flavor of the day. It's always just one flavor. But there's no set schedule. You don't walk down Lexington towards Orange from Arthur J's thinking, Tuesday so it must be lime, Wednesday so it's cherry. You never know. Around Mansfield it hits you—though strawberry carries farther, who knows why—and you gulp it in all Tangerine, Yeah! Or Right on, Grape! You can't help but flex your smile muscles, it's something Disneyland should do. And best of all it's steam from the Jell-O vats venting, I guess, so it lingers all night long, but it's not a factory like Ford or Lockheed where one shift leaves and another comes on and they keep making Jell-O till death do us part. It's strictly 9-to-5. After hours, those steps are mine.

All mine.

Hell fuckin na.

Though it sounds like I've got company tonight. Cornering onto Orange from Lexington I hear singing, chicks singing, and even when I con the dots from the "Sweet Home Alabama" sound of one of them I'm all What the fuckety-fuck indeed, because I've heard "Pretty Vacant" on the streets around here lately and "Billie Jean" and that awful "Voulez-vous Couchez avec Moi" song and even "My Way," but never anything like this.

*Flies in the buttermilk,*
*Shoo fly shoo,*
*Flies in the buttermilk,*
*Shoo fly shoo,*
*My fly's open, how about you?*
*Strip to my Lou, my darling.*

It's Squid and Siouxsie. They're whores and dykes and tweakers, they're both fifteen. And I figure they're faced on Mad Dog they're so outta control, but Siouxsie plants a big wet one on me when I top the steps and I don't smell anything on her breath but an Oki Dog, that's two hot dogs, a piece of American cheese, chili, and pastrami rolled up in a tortilla, a real feast fit for a Pilgrim in other words, not to mention the youth of today, because at Oki's they won't let you order anything else, if you ask for, say, a teriyaki burrito, they always go, "No! Punk rock! Oki Dog and fries!" But anyways the lezzie byrds must not be tweaking either, not with appetites.

"It's not FAIR," Siouxsie yells up to the Jell-O gods, like the steps are the stage at the Greek Theatre and she doesn't want tightwads up in the trees past the fences to miss a single word, she doesn't want heshers partying at the Hollywood sign to miss a single word, she doesn't want homies in fuckin South Pasadena to miss a single word, "You're a BOY. And YOUR skin's softer than HERS."

She all-falls-down laughing on the step beside me and Squid reaches over and brushes my cheek with her fingers and tells Siouxsie she's whorely mistaken, it's fuzz, not skin, I'm fuzzy as a Georgia peach, or Jaw-ja is how she actually says it, she's got what she calls her magnolia drawl going, she came out here from Tuscaloosa after her wicked stepmother raided her record collection and subbed Tony Orlando for Talking Heads and Debby Boone for Lydia Lunch.

"Rockets here's a Norelco virgin."

"Unlike a certain you-know-what-bian I know," Siouxsie says, and they're in female mud wrestling mode before you can say Steve and Melody Live at the Hollywood Tropicana, Squid pins Siouxsie on the brick patio above the steps and the tag-team tickling lasts until there's just enough breath left between them to start singing again, second verse, tweaked as the first.

*Lost my partner, who'll I screw?*

*Lost my partner, who'll I screw?*

*Back door's open, guess it'll do*

*Strip to my Lou, my darling.*

So I tell them I get it now, back door action, woo hoo hoo and boo hoo too for you and you, but they're all no no no, that part was strictly verbal. And they say the scene itself was strictly hetero, though when I finally get the play-by-play of the play-for-pay it's not what that Crystal Cathedral dude would call the straightest story ever told. They score the trick on Sunset by the IHOP and first he takes them up to C.C. Brown's Ice Cream Parlor on Hollywood Boulevard, where the cashier sits reading the Book of Job at the register and the waitresses are all grannies on steroids who've worked there since the Age of Steam. And Squid and Siouxsie let him know the peter meter's running, but he's set on buying them banana splits, and except for telling them to smack their lips every now and then while they chew the Chiquita there's no real clue how he floats his battle wagon till they get to his apartment on Franklin afterwards, and there's a sandbox in the living room.

And a Playskool record player complete with carrying handle and a stack of colored vinyl 45s beside it on the coffee table that are nothing but nursery rhymes and Mousketeer anthems and teddy bear marches, all on the Magic Kingdom label.

And shrink-wrap packs of white cotton panties, girls size Large.

So they change into their nice new undies, in the powder room he calls it, since naturally he's the kind of old-school gentleman who wouldn't dream of watching, oh my no. And then he spreads a towel on the sofa and strips to his Y-fronts and sits there playing DJ with one hand and hammering his hamster with the other while Squid and Siouxsie skip around the sandbox jiggling their titties and belting out his smutty changes on kindergarten's greatest hits.

For an hour.

For two hundred bucks.

And there's more where that came from if they'll dye their hair normal and wear it in pigtails.

"Five bills," says Squid. "And he doesn't even touch us."

*Cat's in the cream jar, ooh, ooh, ooh,*

*Cat's in the cream jar, ooh, ooh, ooh,*

*Slice of hair pie, I'll take two,*

*Strip to my Lou, my darling.*

I tell them we could add a rocking beat to that.

"Who's we?" Siouxsie says.

"I mean Bosco, mostly. He said he might start a band. I might help, learn keyboards or something."

They both laugh.

"It ain't a joke band!"

But they say the joke's on me, if Bosco's fronting it, and true he is like a man with a past in the scene here, band-wise, a shitty past, when I met him he was in SSharx, they used to sniff a lot of paint, they were that kind of band. And their drummer's mom worked for the state I guess, and she got them a gig at a mental hospital down in San Diego, it was supposed to be like therapy. For the patients, I mean. And I went along. And in the middle of the set Bosco got bored because no one was moving, so he did a split jump and fell sideways onto the floor and choked himself with the mic chord and smashed himself in the head with the mic, and the boys in white coats just started wheeling the audience back to their rooms. And later he told me he heard afterwards that most of them thought they were the Beach Boys, but they all had a really good time.

"So where's Bosco now?"

I tell Siouxsie he's over at Arthur J's, and just like that they're back in Playskool mode, a bawk-bawk here and a bawk-bawk there, here a bawk, there a bawk, everywhere a bawk-bawk, it's the main chickenhawk hang in Hollywood, along with the Gold Cup up on Las Palmas. I used to live there practically, it was like a meal ticket, craving elderqueers would buy me burgers just to talk to me, but now I've got the lifetime ban for sneaking in the back and peeing in the ice-maker on a double dare from Tony the Hustler.

"Don't you reckon Bosco's looking more like a rooster to those daddies nowadays?" Squid says.

"He's only a year older than you guys."

"On that corner sixteen's retirement age," Squid says.

So I'm all Same goes double for you with Mr. Slice of Hair Pie, you'd better cash in while you can. And she tells me not to worry my spiky little head none, they'll be back in the sandbox before I can say Old Snatch-Donald Had a Farm.

And they'll be rich.

And they'll party down.

So I ask them what they're on tonight anyways, and it turns out it's MDA.

"Want some?" Siouxsie asks.

"Maybe later."

"When y'all have got company, you mean?" Squid says.

"I've got company now."

"Not the kind of company you want for the Loooovvvvve Drug, white sugar."

I say I don't need company like that, they're not the only ones who already scored tonight, I've been around the block myself, not once but twice, and of course they want every nasty detail, though they don't think sex between guys is disgusting, they just think it's hilarious. So I tell them first off I got twenty-five, just for showing my feet to a nelly nigger, what happened was, this black guy caught Bosco's eye in the parking lot at Arthur J's, and Bosco made the connect and called me over, and I stood there leaning into his window while he gave me the once over twice. And then it went as usual, I'm not a cop from him and I don't do anything from me, till he was all, "I'm into feet. Young men's feet."

I just shrugged like I'd been hearing it since I was in Pampers, I am a poseur and I don't care, though if any part of me is like the last priority of any stranger I ever met, it's gotta be my feet. I mean my belly button's a social butterfly compared to my feet, I've had major label interest there for years.

So that's when the collective bargaining started, because he wanted to check out my feet to see if he could use them, and I said For what, and he said for photographs, he was a photographer, and this is Hollywood, remember, so even year one little babies at the Braille Institute can see the feature presentation, I show him my feet, Nah, sorry, not what I'm looking for, later days, and faster than it takes a third grader to find the titties in the latest National Geographic he's parked in Citrus Alley, drooling over sweet memories and flogging his ferret twice as hard because he put one over on a white boy.

So I shook my head and stepped back from the window and just like that he started talking twenty, for a quick look-see. And I wasted less than zero time, his or mine, I swung one foot up onto the doorframe and reached down to unlace and the next thing you know the guy's checking into Seizure World, choking out "Not here! Not here!" like I wagged my wenus at him instead of my Monkey Boot.

Then he tells me to get in, and though I know I'll never do the deed napoleon solo still I stop to A the Q whether I would if he was white, and decide I probably would if he wasn't a weirdo, which he definitely is, but it's the weird part flashing Warning! Caution! Merging Buses! and not the black part. And then it hits me, he might even be the Strangler.

Hell fuckin na.

But on split-second thought there's just no way unless the Strangler's switched from girls to boys to throw off Homicide. And even if he is, and even if he had, ten to one he'd be waving a bill in the air and promising to suck me harder than a J. Edgar Hoover vacuum, not nickel-and-diming over a toe-check in Citrus Alley.

And besides all that, everyone knows the Strangler picks up his victims on Hollywood Boulevard, and Arthur J's is on Santa Monica.

But what-fuckin-ever, when the talk turns to heels on wheels I let Bosco run with the foot-ball so to speak, and he says we won't butt-plant in anybody's bucket seats for less than twenty-five, and like he means it too. So before you know it I'm folding two bills between my fingers and we're cruising Citrus Alley-ward. And then Bosco's out on the pavement holding the guy's keys as our cover-my-virgin-ass insurance in case he gets a sudden itch to hijack me off to the valley, ever since that bottomfeeder in Reseda made Liewitness News for keeping that fifteen-year-old chick as a sex slave in a box under his waterbed none of us jacks and none of us jills need milk cartons anymore to warn us off the copycats on the dark side of Cahuenga Pass.

So I'm bent over in the passenger seat unlacing, and after all that wind-up I should have known. Brother Nature takes his course and guess who turns out to be separated at birth from Ray Charles, he isn't seeing what he wants to see. But at least I've got presidents on paper in the change pocket of my jeans. And then he's pulling out his wallet for an encore, but instead of a tip for my trouble I end up palming a business card, I wonder if it means he's on call in case my feet do the Cinderella thing.

But wait.

Another card.

Plastic this time.

Slapped down in my hand just long enough for me to run a finger over the cutout-line of a detachable key before he snatches it back, peels the fucker off, says it's courtesy of Triple A, and fits it into the ignition.

And turns over the engine while I sit there slow-motion fumbling for the door handle inside and Bosco dives for it fast motion outside and at the same time the guy's saying in this Father Superior I-showed-you-so voice, "I know you're tough, but you be careful."

"Nick Vogue, Photographer." Bosco reads off the card like he's puking poison after I fall into his arms out the door of the car and the guy peels out towards Santa Monica Boulevard while I'm taking ocean-as-in-Marianas-Trench-deep breaths and wondering what the fuck I'm doing anyways and what the fuck comes next in the year of our bored 1981 when screeching weasel wheels I remember what comes next is my birthday and I mean literally, as soon as tomorrow turns into today. And when I tell Bosco he's all Hell fuckin na, dude, there's only one way to celebrate, and he laughs this double hiccup laugh he lifted from some old timer we heard on a rockabilly comp one time at Disgraceland, and sings that line from the Adolescents song "Kids of the Black Hole" about the nights of birthdays, the nights of fry, and before you can say the nights of endless drinking, the knights of violence, the nights of noise he's planting a clove cigarette in an Oki Dog for me as a candle while I've got these drool icicles forming at the corners of my mouth like a fuckin St. Bernard, waiting to skarf, I've been lagging in all major food groups since that king-size box of Good-n-Plenty's yesterday sometime, yesterday pretty early, actually. And then we're walking up Highland towards Selma on the lookout for this dealer he knows named Radar, who's supposed to have some Vitamin L.

And we find him too, on the steps of the church on Selma near the corner of Wilcox, and he's got what we're looking for.

Tabs.

But he'll only sell a sheet. A hundred tabs. Two hundred bucks. Blue dragons. Premium fry.

"I ain't small timin' anymore. Cops catch you with goods and a pocketful of ones and they slam you with sales. Sales to kids. And you're kids. Take it or leave it."

"Front me," Bosco says.

Radar just laughs. "In your wet dreams. Work the Spotlite. Two blowjobs'll cover it. Go drain your balls. I'll be around."

I know the Spotlite, but I've never been inside. It's a hustler bar on the corner of Selma and Cahuenga. There's a back bar where older punks would hang out sometimes after the LAPD shut down the Masque. I heard there's an X song on the jukebox. I ask Bosco what it's like.

"Dark."

He says it's so dark that when you first walk in you can't see anything at all. It's long and narrow and there's booths on one side and the bar on the other and you open the door and everyone can see you but you can't see them. Kind of like walking out on stage.

Into the spotlight.

Heh heh heh.

Only the bartender's front and center in the audience, so he proofs you on autopilot.

We're almost to Cahuenga. Bosco decides to cruise inside anyways and get the boot.

"Sometimes guys see you and follow you out. Maybe we'll get lucky."

He says "we" so I'm right beside him crossing Selma and pushing through these heavy leather curtains that hang in front of the real door. But then he stops and turns to me and says, "I don't know, man. Maybe you'd better—"

The door opens inwards and low voices carry out in the draft with the beer smell and smoke. The music on the box definitely isn't X. Someone burly elbows sideways past us and then the voices stop inside. I figure that's my cue to back my way out and prop up the stucco wall, facing Cahuenga. Bosco lasts maybe a minute more inside. He says he faked looking for ID so his eyes could adjust, and he saw this guy he knows, and the guy saw him too, and he thinks he might be coming outside, so I'd better chill around the corner, two of us tandem might scare him off.

"He's a good trick. One-fifty. Fully non-sexual."

So I switch to propping up the Selma wall, but thirty seconds over Little Tokyo later Bosco's grabbing my arm and steering me down the sidewalk doubletime while he's hissing in my ear.

"He saw you in the doorway and he likes you, man. We'll go up to his house. It's just on Camrose. I'll wait right outside. You don't have to do anything. Just watch TV."

"But—"

"It doesn't matter. It's like following a script. I told him you're really shy and you've never done this shit before and you and me need to talk before you go inside. Don't worry. Everything's cool."

He turns me around before I get a word out and the guy's waiting for us on the corner. Bosco says, "Bill, this is my little brother. Sid."

I stick out my hand.

"Sid, this is Bill. The Dog Groomer to the Stars."

The house is only like ten blocks away, up towards Hollywood Bowl, but Bosco gets Bill to spring for a cab by saying we're supposed to meet our sister by eleven at Crossroads of the World for some clubbing action, and otherwise we'll keep her waiting. Bill asks, "What's her name?" and Bosco elbows me, we're all in the back seat and he's in the middle.

"Nancy."

I do a face-check with the back of my hand for grin camo, then it hits me that Bosco never told me what his name's supposed to be, and I wonder what's up with the fake name shit anyways, since we all made ours up in the first place, no, just kidding, it says Rockets Redglare right here on my Social Insecurity card.

Bill says he doesn't get out on the town as much as he might wish. He's got this way of talking that reminds me of people with English accents, not punks of course but the respectable ones, except without the sound of the accent itself. It's hard to describe. Suave, I'd guess you call it. When he pays the fare he says to the cabbie, "And a very pleasant evening to you," like he's cruising into the opera in a tux with a babe in a ballgown on either arm instead of heading for the Betamax and the California king with a couple of punk rock rent boys in tow.

The cabbie just grunts. He picked us up on Selma, after all. I wonder what he thinks we'll do with Bill.

Work him over with our studded belts?

Pee on him in his bathtub?

Force-feed him dog biscuits?

Those are all Donny stories. I've never done anything like that. The closest was last year staying at Skinhead Manor by Hollywood High. It was right after Sham 69 played the Whisky and we all had shaved heads and combat boots, and Eugene started scoring these tricks with Jews and minorities who got their kinks out through abuse by skinheads, not physical but verbal. And I got in on a few of those, they'd pay extra for a whole crew of us. I thought it would be creepy, but basically it cracked me up. I mean none of us were white power or even very prejudiced, the Stern brothers who rented the house were Jews themselves, so we really had to work it to be all hard and mean, and when this one black guy tried to get us telling darky jokes we couldn't even think of any. So instead we made up a song on the spot with Jonny Two Bags on guitar and Bosco on bass called "I Hate

Niggers," and that was such a hit we did an encore later for this high-roller Jewish movie agent, "Anne Frank was a Bitch."

That's not Bill's thing though. Not even. We jam up the walk and he goes inside and closes the door while we stand on the porch and Bosco runs it down for me. It sounds pretty easy. But I guess "non-sexual" just means the trick keeps his hands to himself and you don't do anything, because I'll be stripping down to my shorts at least and our buddy Bill will be choking his cheetah like the night before the world's end as long as I stick to the script. And I can't help feeling kind of sketch about being in a strange house almost naked with a stranger alone in his bedroom, so I ask Bosco why he can't go in too.

"He wants one on one. I'll be right here. I already told him the door stays unlocked. If he tries anything weird, just yell."

He starts to knock, but I grab his hand.

"Just go in with me, okay? Walk me back to the bedroom."

"Sure. Okay. We gotta move, though. You ready?"

"Wait. You didn't tell me. Do I have to get a hard-on?"

"NO!"

The house smells like lemon-wax furniture polish and jasmine coming in through open windows. No sign of any dogs. Walking down the straight-shot hallway to the bedroom Bill says something about his lover who died. In the bedroom he lights a scented candle while I settle down on the end of the bed.

Bosco spike-checks my hair with the palm of his hand and says, "Have fun."

I get a little panicked hearing his Docs stomp off down the hall. Bill closes the door and says, "Please make yourself comfortable, Sid. I want you to feel at home."

Bosco told me that's the hint to show some skin. I hunch over and unlace my boots. Then peeling off my jeans I feel the folded bills from Nick Vogue Photographer in my change pocket. And that reminds me of the first rule of hustling.

Money up front.

The rule you never break.

Everybody knows that.

But I can't ask him. Not now.

I never thought I'd be this spooked. I don't know what to do with my jeans, so I drop them on the floor. I pull off my socks. I wonder what the fuck is wrong with my feet. Why didn't that guy like them?

I sit back up and Bill puts a little pinner joint in my hand. He lights it for me. And it's some raspy shit, it tastes fuckin awful, but I'm grateful, maybe it'll calm me down. I try to pass it back, and he says, "It's all for you."

So I burn it down while Bill gets comfortable, too. He says his dressing gown is silk from Thailand.

"Thailand's a wonderful country, Sid. I think you'd like it there."

I tell him I've never even been to Tijuana and he makes this tsking sound and says my whole life's ahead of me and he's sure I'll make something of myself. Though he doesn't say what.

## The MacMillan Hair

### Heidi Julavits

The plain trouble was this: behind the Lizard family's house, all the lawns ran together like a parched brown flood. In front there were adobe-styled mailboxes and complimentary pink pebbles instead of grass, in front there were black roads coming from practically nowhere and concluding at a pumice-crete utility shed, but behind it all there was nothing but land with a breathtaking history of struggle and triumph.

Babbitt watched their stepdad's satellite TV and knew about things. Land with a breathtaking history of struggle and triumph, Babbitt explained to his siblings (translating from the New Utah Development brochure), is land without trees or animals or water or fences; it's land where people fly in from the coast to shoot lonely car commercials because it's cheaper than dropping a nuclear bomb closer to home.

Dibs, the littlest Lizard except for the triplets, added: it makes a person feel unhinged, all those missing things. The Lizards typically felt queasy and undone after they'd roamed so far from home in search of something confining, an ocean, maybe, that they couldn't hear the dinner threats their mother Sal bellowed atop the new fake well in the backyard.

I hope your dinner's spit-gluey and cold by the time you get back, Sal would yell, kicking at the new fake well bucket where the squirrels fornicated. I hope you get a corn niblet caught in your throat. I hope you gag on a pudding skin.

Babbitt suggested to their stepdad, Big, that maybe a fence might be a good idea. Big worked at the tourist rodeo and his scarred-up face knew about fences intimately.

I'm thinking about marauders, said Babbitt, squinting over the plains. I'm just thinking ahead to darker times.

Big always had his hands in Babbitt's hair like he was looking for a pretend lost thing.

You're too damned thoughtful, Big chided, ruffling Babbitt's hair. You know what I worried about at your age? Tackle equipment. Who'd stole it, was it rusting, stuff of that nature. But maybe you want to know how babies are made?

Babbitt shook his head.

A boy needs rules, Babbitt explained. A boy needs limitations or he might wear himself out before he's hardly ten.

Well then, Big said, I command you to keep your pants on. No fussing in those danderpatches, or a whipping I'll design for you the likes of which you'll thank me for.

Babbitt smiled at Big, humored the man, who could no sooner whip him than make their mother less sad.

Babbit featured the ongoing boundary dispute with the MacMillan neighbors in the Lizards' inaugural and ultimate issue of The New Utah Daily Herald International Tribune Intelligencer.

On the nearer side of twilight, Tuesday, a mute four year old known as Bud MacMillan roamed southward or so of the exhaust pipe marking Blanco's grave, and was struck upon his dumb head by one Polly Lizard with what appeared, by some accounts, to be a roof tile.

Notice you didn't mention how he's unhearing and baby-sized! protested an older MacMillan (they came in all sizes, the MacMillans—Older, Wide, Skinny, Baby). Notice you didn't mention how you can't go through life hitting deaf babies with rocks!

Notice it's only his ears that don't work, Polly said, rubbing her tile. He can goddamned see where he's going.

Don't coddle the handicapped, Dibs advised. You'll make him deeply useless.

This is one-sided crap, said the Older MacMillan. He ripped up the inaugural and ultimate issue of The New Utah Daily Herald International Tribune Intelligencer. He blew his nose in it. He shoved it down his pants and fake farted on it.

The Seven MacMillans ranged in size, this was true, but they all shared an identical rug-like orangish hair. It banished any light that shone on it; it was tufted and prickly on boys, braided and prickly on girls. It was terrible hair, more like a substance that has been regurgitated from a river and dried to a lifeless fiber on a rockflat. The MacMillans envied the Lizards their soft puppy heads, heads that strangers rubbed in passing to remind themselves of less sentient times. The MacMillans would rip it from the Lizards' skulls whenever the two families met up for picnics or simply by accident in the mindless forever behind their houses. They collected this hair in an old thermos. The wide girl MacMillan braided the Lizard hair into anklets that her brothers and sisters wore under their socks. She told Polly that she was making a hair cape for each of her brothers and sisters, so that their bodies could be more touchable.

Such a literal family I've barely encountered the likes of, Polly said, scratching under her stocking cap, notice I'm not saying stupid. The Lizards wore suntan stockings on their heads, nicked from Sal's underwear drawer. The stockings were still the shape of Sal's feet, her toes and heels kicking from the tops of their heads. Like roosters, Big said. Like Indians, Dibs said. Like idiots, Polly said. The stockings kept what hair they had left close to their scalps, because they never knew when a MacMillan might lurch from behind a bush, and set upon them with his freckly ripping fists.

The elastic turned their foreheads blue.

Babbitt suggested that a boundary might be established between the lawns to contain the unrest. He actually said contain the unrest, which Dibs misunderstood, because he did not care for the satellite news quite like Babbitt did, that the MacMillans had a contagious sickness that caused sleeplessness. This did not surprise him, because they were so goddawful white beneath their orange hair. They had a sickness and did not respond properly to night.

We will dig a trench, Dibs commanded.

This was easily done. The trench was not straight; it respected the single, unflowering cactus bush, it respected the grave of Blanco, the MacMillan's former ferret, it respected the natural to-and-fro of the land that had once been food for some lumbering, fenced-in animal. Babbitt and Polly dug with rectangular silver snow shovels; Dibs followed behind them, pocketing the skull-shaped mushrooms that grew in the earth. He put these mushrooms into jars. They had little brown hairs; they looked like voodoo heads.

The MacMillans watched from behind an old golf cart their father'd been planning to fix since the flood. They bulleted old golf balls from a stiff knit bag in the back of the cart. They encouraged Bud to pull his elastic pants aside and piss with the wind, covering the Lizards with a light rank spray.

I hereby proclaim this land divided, Babbitt said, wielding his silver shovel. It caught the sunshine and was hurtful to observe.

The MacMillans slunk from behind the golf cart, their white hands over their whiter faces. They threw more golf balls. They shuffled closer to the trench.

I say this land, Babbitt repeated, swinging the shovel like a scythe—has been divided.

The MacMillans ducked and skittered. They all took shelter behind the golf cart except for Bud. He stared at Polly and moved his lips as he was accustomed to doing, chewing at the air but making nary a sound, not even so much as a gargle. Dibs figured that Bud ate sound, and for that reason he was a useful presence in their neighborhood, which was bounded to the north by a truck artery and loud in the night. Polly reached over the trench like she might hit the quiet little man. Instead she grabbed a single, coiling strand of his orange hair. She jerked with her quick wrist. She pushed the hair in front of Bud's shiny, empty mouth like a word she'd pulled from his brain. She paraded along the trench waving the hair over her stockinged head, to prove to the MacMillans, beyond a faithful doubt, that their age of influence had hastened to a close.

Since the procuring of the MacMillan Hair, domestic relations at the Lizard house had devolved nicely. Big suddenly stopped caring about being a special stepdad and sloggered into being a plain old man, skimming the grocery supplements next to the white noise machine. Sal grew listless and hardly worried when the Lizards roamed as far as the pudding plant. The plant parking lot was lined with blue trash receptacles, where the plant people disposed of their clear plastic masks after work. Some of these masks had lipstick on the inside. Polly liked to wear a lipsticky mask and sit astride Dibs, also wearing a mask. They would press their mask faces together and Babbitt would make suctiony noises against his forearm to hide the sound of all that plastic cricking and dinging in a most unromantic way. By the time they got home, Sal was knitting by the white noise machine and Big was OUT BEING USEFUL which meant he was FETCHING SALVE FOR YOUR MOTHER'S POOR HANDS. She would hold out her palms next to her face as though she might ooze tears from their withery middles. The Lizards high-fived her as they strode past her to their rooms. Her hands were chapped and icy to the touch, as though she'd been lost in a blizzard.

All and all, Polly said, things seemed somewhat back to normal. By normal she meant Before He Left, because He had set the standard for fiery neglect. Then He'd gone, and Big took His place, all worked up to be likable. Big mucked up their sandwiches with old family jams, he sang as he scrubbed the syrupy dishes, he acted like their most miserably cramped moments were enough to make him yodel with a kind of domestic ecstasy.

You haven't seen what lonely I've seen, he'd say, sitting on end of their wooshy mattresses, crunching their toes with his bony bottom. Riding horses up high like I do, I've seen old water in the air. I've seen clear through the tops of ladies heads. I've seen terrible things only the sun can see.

You've seen down ladies dresses, you pervy old beanpole, Polly would say, kicking upward with her feet, feeling the sharp places where her stepdad's legs fused together inside his stiff rodeo pants. Now get the heck off my bed.

No matter how much they ignored Big, he kept trying to humiliate them by being useful. He bleached out stains that had been on their knee-length sweatshirts since Before He Left. He tried to erase dark things they had counted on as permanent.

Since the procuring of the MacMillan Hair, however, Big had stopped bothering. He stole the fatty scraps off their plates and left the dishes until morning. He didn't tell them stories about the rodeo, where he barely hung onto his job. He disappeared every night in search of bodily necessities for their mother, salves for her hands or a poultice for her sagging face. The Lizards did as they pleased, and nobody touched them or wished them sweet dreams with a phony voice that went down-up-down SWEET DREE-EEMS, nobody showered them with insincere munificence—in short, nobody took them anymore for fools.

Best was that Big and Sal stopped trying to outlove them. This had been the most disturbing development After He Left. Even His Leaving couldn't compare to all the love that battered the insides of their little house, gouging out sheetrock and knocking pictures off walls. Big moved in and she competed with him to do their laundry, she competed with him to do their dishes, she competed to sit on their beds at night, she said SWEET DREE-EEMS louder and louder until the squirrels abandoned their nests in the walls. The Lizards woke up to the smell of sugar and soap, they woke up to the noisy, stinking efforts of love on their behalf. It made them nervous. Dibs developed chronic pains in his chest; Polly got a rash. They listened to their mother yelling at night to LEAVE MY LIZARDS BE, and Big would somberly say it was USELESS TO FIGHT WITH HER

OVER HER POOR, POOR LIZARDS, like they were already raised on too much ruin to be considered much better than dead.

Then Sal stopped using her white noise machine, because suddenly it was important for her to listen, even though listening made her sick. When He was around, she'd hear too much and have to take to her bed. He bought her the white noise machine, and her health improved. The Lizards missed the white noise machine, more than they missed Him. It covered up the air uglinesses they were so incapable of quelling, the air uglinesses that made Sal knit faster and faster, her needles producing a sound not unlike that of a wolverine gnashing her teeth.

Since the procuring of the MacMillan Hair, however, the white noise machine had been unearthed from beneath its quilted cozy; it was plugged in where the TV had been, in front of the bricked-in fireplace. It was turned on ECON HIGH, because there were nighttime blackouts that left the house dark and hot and hearable. Worst were the hearable noises of Big and Sal so-called loving each other. The worst kind of lying, Polly would say. Makes me sicker than a cat.

The MacMillan Hair was stored in a jar that Dibs kept under the hood of His busted gas grill. This jar had been the home to various other treasured items, namely

a bullet

a grasshopper

a casino token (truck flattened)

a bird skull

a big toenail (Sal's)

a scab (Babbitt's)

a maybe pearl, maybe small white stone

These treasured items had brought the family waves of better luck from time to time, but their powers diminished when Dibs forgot to think about the jar every day at the stroke of noon. The gong of the nearby churchbell, he eventually surmised, was wrapped in baffling for religious reasons on the first Monday of every month, and did not ring. On these days he forgot to think of the jar, fixing it in his head, floating in blackness or sometimes blueness or sometimes yellowness, depending on his mood, the bullet-grasshopper-token-skull-nail-scab-pearl surrounded by an orbit of light that expanded and contracted like a clear heart. Always after this slip of the mind their lives would turn unpredictable. Sal would want to hear about their digging projects. Babbitt's satellite would get shorted out by a bird. He would leave or He would come back or He would leave again.

Since the procuring of the MacMillan hair, Dibs had been tireless in his remembering. He instituted a midnight policy, setting an alarm in order to remember the hair—with its spiky end and its white bulb follicle beginning, with its tensile strength of wire—exactly twice a day. Polly complained and Babbitt beat him with a pillow. But Dibs said BE WARY WHAT YOU DISDAIN, PEOPLE, and they stopped disdaining him and his mysterious habits; he was the weather forecaster in the family, and he could call up clouds or sun or water or night, it seemed, with his divining principles that no one understood.

The MacMillan Hair was so powerful, Dibs felt, that it was possible even that He might return. This was not necessarily to be desired, but it did feel possible. He talked to Polly and Babbitt and the others who were too small to have much of an opinion, the triplets Chigger, Means, and Poquot, who loved to burble their lips and listen.

Things were more predictable when he was around, Polly said cautiously, notice I'm not saying better.

Better wetter wigger wog said Poquot.

Comebacks are for wafflers, said Babbitt. He kicked at a rock.

Polly accused Babbitt of favoring Big, because he took him fishing and bequeathed him a pocketful of Big Family lures.

Lewders in the sewders said Means.

Lollalalalalallo said Chigger.

I'm saying it's best to be prepared for anything, Dibs said. Last thing we need is a shock, People. It'll throw us off our game.

They agreed to be prepared for anything. Dibs required all of them, even the triplets, to sign the Official Release Form which Dibs would present to Him upon his return.

Best He knows He's free to go, Dibs said.

Nothing worse for the morale of a family than to have a bald man coming and going, Polly said.

Chigger, Means, and Poquot gargled in agreement. Polly wiped their triply flying spit off her calves.

There was nothing, however, that might have prepared them for Sal's new hairdo. She came home a few days later from Hilde's Salon with a terrible mind to look pretty.

What the, Polly said.

Sal had dyed her hair a MacMillany red. It was pinned up tight and waxed glossy like a dining room table.

Notice I didn't ask your opinion, Sal said, wooshing her hips back and forth as she put away the groceries. She bent low and kissed Polly on the head. It's high time we made you less Lizard-like, she said, hauling on Polly's dragging sweatshirt, so dragging it might have been a thick cottony habit. I'll take you to Hilde tomorrow and see what kind of girl-hope she can drum out of you.

The next afternoon, Polly hid behind the receptacles in the plant parking lot, but Sal found her anyway.

Take off that damned mask, she said, as she drove to the salon. She pronounced it SAH-LOW, in the French Persuasion. Do you know where that mask has been? Do you?

Hilde smiled at Polly and rubbed her soft head and said my my she looks just like Him now, doesn't she poor fish, snapping a black trashbag bib around Polly's neck.

Sal tried to pull the mask off Polly's face but Polly fell out of the chair and pretended she couldn't breath.

Hell, just let her wear it, Hilde said, approaching Polly with her metallic blue scissors.

On the car ride home, Polly cried into her mask and rendered it gummy. Sal took long side looks at Polly with her short stiff hair and her pins and said you look just like a lady. Might just make something useful out of you yet.

BUFF FYE TOO, Polly spat.

Just like me, Sal concurred.

Polly didn't reply. Instead she mouthed words inside her mask, talking soundlessly to herself in the spirit of little mute Bud MacMillan. I'M NOT ONE HAIR LIKE YOU, she mouthed into her mask. She realized how much more responsible it was to talk when the only person who had to hear you was yourself.

NOT ONE HAIR, Polly mouthed, YOU DAFT KNITTING LAYABOUT.

It was Dibs who discovered that the MacMillan Hair was missing.

Stoled I presume, he said, his eyes trawling long over the trench and Blanco's grave to the golf cart and the MacMillan house beyond. Can't be certain, of course, until the Committee files its report. The MacMillan lawn was empty, had been empty for weeks. The MacMillan kids, when they saw them at school, were cowering and clumped together like old noodles. Teachers kept a safe distance and whispered over their travel mugs TROUBLES IN THE HOME.

Babbitt said he knew about the troubles, or at least, from his satellite watching, he could ascertain. I ascertain civil uprisings in the MacMillan Strip, Babbitt said. I ascertain a low pressure zone originating in the Western MacMillans.

Polly said she'd seen the Mrs. MacMillan crying in the golf cart. She'd seen her put a golf ball in her mouth and examine her round white OOOH in the cart's rearview mirror. She'd seen the Mrs. MacMillan pour water down the exhaust pipe onto the body of Blanco, like he was a plant and she was watering him.

Lady can't contain her unrest, Dibs said.

Polly didn't say what she suspected, that the Mr. MacMillan had a shine on Sal, and Sal had a shine on him. Sal was very obvious, her desires were color-coded and easier to read than a baboon's bottom. She dyed her hair like the men she wanted to attract, and always it worked, the two people matching themselves up like animals. Polly had seen it before, she'd watched her mother change her colors before. This was how she made herself feel useful. He was totally bald, He was never one she could match unless she shaved herself clean like a nun. He had left her and she was relieved, now she could keep her hair forever and stop feeling badly that she couldn't find a purpose when he was around.

But Polly kept her mouth shut. There were necessary quiets between the Lizards, because Dibs believed Sal's head was noise-ruined after living on a truck artery with noisy children and noisy neighbors, and this fueled his need to make the house safely neglectful with his stones and his skulls and his jars.

Unrest be damned, Dibs said. We must activate the Holy Hair Recovery Committee.

Dibs put double-sided sticky tape on the hands and feet of the triplets, whom he commanded to walk on all fours in increasingly large circles around the gas grill. He examined their woolly hands and feet, picking through the twigs and grass and insects.

Nothing, he reported at bedtime. The Holy Hair Recovery Committee feels it can confidently state its findings: this was no goddamned accident.

Dibs gave Polly the Committee-Issue Holy Hair Recovery Goggles, which would make the MacMillan hair appear a bright,

bright blue if she spotted it. The glasses were Sal's gold reading specs, the lenses replaced with black paper into which a sewing needle had been inserted then removed. They only worked at night. After the house had gone to bed, Polly walked out past the grill in her nightgown and sweatshirt and put on the Holy Hair Recovery Glasses. She bungled her way around the yard, following her pinprick vision. She saw dark and dark and more dark, which she would report back to the Committee. Darned things are worth a damned darn, she'd tell them.

She didn't realize that she had crossed the trench until she kicked the soft tire of the golf cart.

Polly fell forward, bracing herself on the sun-crackled seat vinyl. She slid into the passenger seat and stared forward through the broken windshield toward the floodlights on the MacMillan porch. The two pricks became like night stars she could make wobble if she threw her head around. She put her hands on the dash and she chased Him down. She dodged trucks carrying milk to the coast, she made good time and could see His bald head like a daytime planet trailing through the wheat. He had never liked her much, so it was easy to follow Him against his wishes, it was easy to swing a silver golf club like a thresher and try to topple off His head to slow Him down. She clenched her hands around a pretend graphite twenty iron, borrowed from the Mr. MacMillan. To herself she mouthed the word FORE. To herself she mouthed the words FASTER FASTER. In her left ear, she felt a wet, fleshy wind.

Her pinprick eyes moved sideways until all she saw was blue. It hurt her brain.

She pulled off the goggles given to her by the Holy Hair Recovery Committee pressed her thumbs into her eyes. She blinked. In front of her was an entire head of holy hair. Bud MacMillan sat behind the wheel of the golf cart in his nightshirt, mouthing words at her.

Polly reached up and smoothed his rough, gnarly, orangey pelt. She kept her hand on his skull and could feel the backwards shooting wind of his talking as it bounced around inside his own skull.

Polly rubbed his daft, holy head. At the bottom of her mean self, Polly just wanted people to stop worrying. She heard everything Sal couldn't hear, because everything had to be heard by somebody. The Lizards split up the listening in the house so that Sal wasn't run down by noises and forced to take to her bed—Babbitt heard the trucks passing, Dibs heard the nature, the triplets heard kitchen noises, she heard the worryings. It was hurting her head to hear the worryings of Dibs and Babbitt. She could steal another Holy Hair to present to the Recovery Committee and the world would quiet up. Same hair, she'd lie, found it under that rock there. Then things would return to normal. Then He might or might not come back. Then Sal would unMacMillan her hair. These goggles are an invaluable gift to science, she'd tell the Committee, who would fund more R&D projects like the one that funded the invention of the Holy Hair Recovery Goggles. Dibs had begun to listen to the satellite news with Babbitt; she knew he'd begun to worry that the committee was under a great deal of fiscal pressure.

Bud MacMillan bounced up and down and he turned the steering wheel, his white tube legs bobbling out from his nightshirt. Polly leaned down and fingered the anklet made of Lizard hair, hidden beneath his gray sock. She undid it and put it into her pocket.

She watched Bud's mouth and tried to see what he was worried about, but there was too much spit and skin. Still, she tried to make sense of him, because she realized as a way of giving up that retards are the messiahs of this world and every hair on their dim heads is a caution against darkness. She put on her Holy Hair Recovery Goggles, because Dibs was always schooling her that LATERAL THINKING IS THE SOUL OF INVENTION. She pressed her two hands into the sides of Bud's bright blue head.

She still couldn't hear, but now she could see what he was saying. She could read it in the blue light that pushed through her pinprick glasses like so much mimeographed newsprint.

He came back, Bud was saying. He stole the Holy Hair.

Who? she asked.

You know who, Lady Girl. The bald man your mother ran off to the coast. And let's not omit the fact He's mad as hell.

Polly stiffened. The thought of Him picking his way through the dug-up lawn, the thought of Him rummaging in his old gas grill for the Holy Hair made her tingle. Before He left He was always scraping the grill clean and feeding the blackened powdered bits of hamburger to his dog, who was a fiend for anything exceedingly dead. That's why He was so angry at them. His dog had choked on the red coil and was colder than Blanco. The Holy Hair had wrapped around his heart like a worm.

That's a matter of opinion, Polly said. Some might say He ran off on account of his own skitchy feet.

He came back and stole the Holy Hair, Bud repeated. The Holy Hair made Him come back.

He stole the hair because it wanted Him to come back?

Of course He wouldn't have come back if he didn't have to. You know how He is, Bud said. He doesn't like to be forced into things, particularly not by His very own Lizards.

Dibs said it was only a possibility, Polly said. We prepared his Release Form. We didn't mean to ask for anything outlandish.

Yeah, but you asked, Bud said. You asked and you know how unattractive asking is, it is goddamned unattractive.

Polly nodded. I know, she said. It's very unattractive.

She squoodged her hands through Bud's hair. Her face was hot and red. She was ashamed that Bud knew about the things she and her brothers stupidly wanted. It hardly made them seem smart enough to know a relic from a piece of trash. In the midst of her embarrassment, Polly found herself wishing she had a pair of plastic masks from the plant so that she and Bud could kiss and make a cricking plastic sound as they talked to themselves inside their own hot protected spaces. She wanted to push her mouth as close to his mouth as possible without actually disturbing his talking, and for this she needed a mask. Kissing without masks was just a meaner way to shut a person up.

Polly put her hands near to Bud's blubbering lips. She almost touched him there, because that was where the true holiness was, it was an unspoken word that couldn't be trapped inside a jar or stolen by a father or eaten by his dog.

Instead she reached high and to the left, she dug her hand into his head and jerked loose from his baby skull a single coiling hair. Through her two needle prick eyes she could see his eyes filling up in the porch lights, she watched them spill over and land onto the cracked steering wheel of the golf cart that the Mr. MacMillan would never fix, just as he would never leave his sleepless wife for any matching-haired neighbor, just as Big would always be somebody's stepdad, just as she and Babbitt and the triplets would feign belief in Dibs's stories about holy stupid things, just as Bud would always be a half-sweet cretin, just as He would keep away no matter what until His teeth fell out like His hair and He was only good for soup. It was the fact of things that was both upsetting and soothing; it was the fact of things that made something like a stupid hair, even a stolen hair, a fake special hair, an outlandishly asking hair, seem like the crucial threshold between bearable and pure unbearableness.

Polly pinched Bud's thigh through his nightshirt and made him cry harder and quieter. His crying sucked a dead quiet over the lawns until even Dibs' worrying and the sound of the trucks was nothing more than far off bug whine. She flipped the Holy Hair Recovery Glasses over her head and pushed the Holy Hair deep into her sweatshirt pocket. She strode back over the trench.

Poor Deaf Bud, she had thought to herself as she pinched his thigh. He was turning out to be an alright, useful little fool.

## Fourteenth Street

### Michelle Tea

I never used the phrase "booty call" in my life—I mean, I just don't talk like that. Being white and over thirty, it would be ridiculous. Darla could call it that, she was younger, she was almost ten years younger then me, and her vocabulary was fascinating. When I called her, at 3 a.m., it was a "booty call." For me, it was simply the erosion of good judgment by time and chemicals.

I was sitting in my living room with the lights blazing against the night outside, three or four girls from the bar sunk into the beat-up couches and armchairs we'd dragged up from the street, ringing the low black coffee table where lines of bad cocaine were being chopped with ATM cards on the tops of CD cases that were permanently dusty and scarred from this very activity.

I was sitting on the worst, most busted-up armchair, the one by the big sliding-glass window that looked out into the backyard where the Filipino headbangers used to sit out all night playing mixed tapes in their boom box which, no shit, was shaped like the grill of a pink Cadillac. The tapes were full of Ozzy and Judas Priest and Megadeth, some classic rock like Journey, but every so often a song would end and the next one would be something totally weird, something from the '80s, Depeche Mode or Gene Loves Jezebel.

In '80s American high school parlance, there was fag music mixed into their righteous heavy-metal tape, and I liked the boys next door even more for not knowing better than to mix the two genres, that mixing such genres where I came from would get your ass kicked. The boys downstairs had played such good, eclectic music that we never minded them playing it, loudly, at like three or four o'clock in the morning. We were generally awake as well and appreciated the soundtrack drifting in through the screen. Also, the boys were total drunks and had more then once caught me and a roommate on our way home from the bar, past last call and beerless, and called us into their yard, waving forty-ounce bottles of Budweiser. They drank the watery brew from Dixie cups, poured over ice.

We would drink with them and marvel at their incredible radio. We'd share our love for Metallica. Returning to our home, me and Jules, my roommate, would talk about how cute they were, especially the one with the mullet, the one who seemed the most dedicated to metal, with concert t-shirts worn soft and fluttering on the scrawny stack of his ribs as he rode around on his dirtbike. We would wonder if they knew we were dykes, or if they were trying to pick up on us. The fact that we were dykes did not cancel our desire for them to desire us. The metalheads next door were so cool, with the little culture they'd created beneath our nighttime windows, and it would be a giant compliment if they wanted to be our boyfriends, even if we had no use for such things.

Fuck it all anyway because those boys, their families, all got evicted because our street, like the rest of the city, is going to shit. Often I had hung my body out my bedroom window and surveyed the view: a chop-shop across the street, whose business is to haul in stolen cars under cover of darkness and disembowel them, selling all the parts for money. All night long the annoying chimes of car alarms siren out from the shop across the street, but you get used to it. I've lived there for years.

Down the street were more auto shops. Leo's on the corner did old cars, cars that could've been classics but they were too messed up. They littered the curb and the sidewalk down there, and were piled high in his lot which was guarded by a great ratty guard dog, its fur a pelt of dreadlocks, all snarls.

There was the corner store, Starshine Market, that I know has a bunch of scams going on. A Lotto scam, I think, and I know for sure their cigarettes are illegal because it says so right on the packs they sold you: *Not for Sale, For Promotional Use Only.*

Then there were other houses like mine, run-down Victorians, though none so blue as mine, none with a stoop so generous, wide and ungated, a great place for drunks to sit and pass out with their bottles, for crackheads to light up their mottled glass pipes, for junkies to peel off a sock and shoot up between their toes. Sometimes packs of young boys would sit there, which was the worst (as packs of young boys always are), though mostly they acted sheepish and cleared the way for me to enter my goddamn house as I approached.

If I looked beyond the immediate warehouses and garages, the horizon is green flanks of overpass in the distance, the sun glinting off the passing cars there. There was the back of the giant hardware store and the tops of a couple of trees. A giant clock that always read 3:35. And running above it all are the webs of electrical wires the buses run on, a thin grid above our heads. It looks like the city's been netted, dragged up from the deep to dry out and die.

That's what I think, leaning out my window, smoking a cigarette and surveying the neighborhood. I breathed easy because this street at least, Fourteenth Street, is a grim strip of slum, avoiding the grip of what the people were calling "gentrification," the march of new restaurants and boutiques that was razing the neighboring boulevards. As long as it stayed away from us we get to keep our houses, our cheap rents, our grimy little nests. And I think, when Fourteenth Street goes, that's when we'll know the city is gone. Watching out my window with my cigarette I felt like a sentry, guarding the city's soul. And then, one day, it's gone.

No, it was piece by piece. First, the empty warehouse across the street, by the chop-shop. One night there's a guy in front of it, a young guy in a plasticky jacket, standing at a podium. I give him a squint. I'm like a small-town landowner or something, some sort of farmer. I don't take kindly to strangers, I think I own the town and what are you doing in it? He's a valet, a car valet. The warehouse, which I always thought was abandoned and maybe up until then was, had its door cracked open and people buzzing around inside. It used to be an art space, a long time ago. I think, maybe it is again. I think that the valet guy is a performance artist. He is doing a public installation, a piece of guerilla street theater about gentrification, about the sudden proliferation of fucking valet parking in our shabby neighborhood. It's a joke. I crack up. Does he really take their cars, I wonder?

"That is so great!" I walk up to him laughing. "That is so smart!"

Fuck, I wish I had thought of it. When am I going to get off my ass and really do something? Something besides drinking and snorting drugs? This guy is an inspiration. He even has that valet parker hairdo, sort of wavy and gelled back. They all have hair like that, the valet parkers. The hairdos of guys who don't really have hairdos but need to look nice so rich people will trust them with their cars. His plasticky windbreaker even says VALET, to make sure everyone gets it.

"I get it!" I gush to this fine artist.

He stays in character. "What are you talking about?" He squints back at me.

"This is great!" I swoop my arm around, bringing in the street, its gutters glittering with broken glass and shiny trash, the decrepit buildings housing illegal operations, the headbangers next door out on their front steps, the tinny sound of 'Crazy Train' tinkling faintly toward us. "Fake valet!"-

"Nah, it's real." The guy shakes his head. He's got that bored thing down pat, that always-bored manner, it's a great defensive posture for extreme urban living. I do it, too, generally, but this fake valet art project knocked it down, got me excited. Except it's not fake. He's a real valet parker and the warehouse behind him is now open for business and that business is throwing huge obnoxious parties for new web sites.

Every weekend, Friday and Saturday, the sun goes down and the place starts buzzing like a hive. The valet parker—who I start screaming at, yelling, "You fucking asshole, valet parking on Fourteenth Street, Jesus!" as if it is his fault, as if he is not just some dude making his dollar—will be there at the curb for about the first month of this problem, but soon the web sites simply start bussing their celebrants in on little shuttles like the kind that circle airports. Because their cars aren't safe here, they get keyed up, the paint curling off in sharp strips, or the windows get smashed just for fun, just for kicks, just to alleviate the stress of watching all these moneyed folks come and treat your home like a big playground.

I knew a girl who was going around pissing on SUVs and documenting it with Polaroids. Once Darla puked on one. Darla. I haven't forgotten her, don't worry. I just want to explain to you the terrain on which our dramatic love was performed. So, the shuttles came depositing these slummers right beneath my window. Once a giant limo, it stretched down our street like some awful tide, like an oil slick.

"Jules, look!" I screamed. We leaned out my window and watched skinny blond girls in tiny dresses emerge giggling from the vehicle's dark insides. Shit.

"Go back to the fucking Marina!" I yelled at them. That's the part of the city they all lived in, I assure you. A fancy area, built on landfill, doomed. That low black coffee table we snort coke from in the living room? Found on the street in the Marina, where me and my last girlfriend would journey for useless couples' counseling. It is visibly of a higher caliber then the rest of our furniture, found on the street in the Mission.

Anyway, the bitches yelled back, we had a great screaming fight, but by the time it occurred to me to throw eggs at them they had retreated into the safety of the web party warehouse, which now seemed to employ a lighting system perhaps borrowed from George Lucas's nearby movie production ranch.

The warehouse vibrated and glowed, punched from the inside with these pulsating, flashing lights, all colors, like a spaceship was stuffed in there. Soon after the warehouse parties started, the Victorian on my corner was bought and renovated, part of the renovation being the obliteration, the literal white-washing of the sloppy but beloved Frida Kahlo mural on its side. No more walking home from the health food store and being greeted by Frida's weary, heavy-browed stare. The ground floor apartment became a restaurant, attempting pathetically to be upscale. They served herb-encrusted rack of lamb, but cut color pictures of the dishes out of magazines and taped them to the windows like the cheapo Chinese cafeterias on Mission Street. It was bound to fail, and until it did we would amuse ourselves by dropping our pants and pissing in the doorway late at night after the bars closed, our bladders heavy with beer. We would relieve ourselves, me and Jules, cackling evil cackles, and then we would join the metalheads for some super-watered-down Budweiser and AC/DC.

And then the metalheads were evicted, and then the speed freaks who ran the neon-sign-making warehouse around the corner were evicted, and then another house was razed and a loft built on the patch of land. And it was over then, our street. The city had found it and it was firmly in its manicured clutches and we who remained were simply biding our time.

Over cocaine and cocktails such were the things we bitched about, the condition of our city, of our neighborhood in particular, which had comforted us, which we had made cooler with our artsy gay white selves, cooler and safer so the theory went, making it fun for less artsy, more straight and wealthy white folks from better neighborhoods to come and fart around for the night like Harlem in the '20s. I could only talk about it for so long without getting frustrated with antsy, coked-out rage.

I thought about Darla. Darla was nineteen and I was thirty, and I was trying to find a balance between responsibility and decadence by spending time with her every other day. It was so anal, but I felt certain that if I saw her more often then it would be the end of me, and I hung on so thinly as it was. I had no fear of corrupting Darla, though I liked to think that I could. It was Darla who would bring me over the edge, who would introduce me to ever more exotic and frowned-upon drugs, Darla who I had the best fucks of my life with, Darla Darla Darla. Like an actual drug I had to ration her lest I spin out of control. Darla who would almost certainly change her name in a year or two, after she adjusted to the amount of Johnnies and Texes and Rickies in the lesbian bar scene, not to mention the girls named Garbage and Sinkhole and Sixteen.

Right now she enjoyed making fun of them, but 'Darla' was no name for a girl like her, with her mean sexy lips and dark eyes and short hair, baggy jeans and sweatshirts and baseball hats. The men who sold her drugs on the corner thought she was a boy, I thought she was a boy, and maybe Darla would even be one of the girls who become a boy, shooting male hormones into the meat of her muscle. Darla was so young still, who knew what she would end up becoming? It excited me to imagine.

Darla was potential, easy to love, simple to project upon. Right now she lived at home and sold pot stolen from her father's medicinal marijuana garden. That was good enough. For now, that was excellent. That was romantic. Coked up at three, four o'clock in the morning, drinking some terrible combination of whatever someone had brought over plus whatever we had in the crusty refrigerator, I would think: Now, why was I being so rigid with Darla? It didn't make sense, it was so silly. She was just a girl, and I was a girl, and it was just fun and not a big deal and why was I depriving us like this?

"You are not fucking a nineteen-year-old," someone in the living room would laugh. Because no one had ever seen her. I had found her on my own, outside the seething, incestuous dyke scene, and I was keeping her to myself.

"Yes, I am," I said. "I am, and she's beautiful. Watch." And I called her. She picked right up. I knew she slept with her phone beside her bed, hoping I would call her.

"Come over," I said. "I have cocaine. Be a teenage boy, sort of an asshole, I'll be your teacher. I'll set up a desk in my bedroom, I'll wear a long pleated skirt, pile my hair on my head."

I would hang up the cordless phone, put it back in its holster, and twenty minutes later she was there. She hung in the living room doorway and was rudely inspected by the others. She was gorgeous, gorgeous like a little bastard that hassles you on the street. I cut her a line. Jules was lamenting the loss of our metalhead neighbors and how we never, not once, had invited them up for a cocktail of scavenged liquor and refrigerator dregs, never offered them a bump or a line, and now they were gone. The girls around the table were now cruising Darla. She sniffed her drugs, hard, and wiped her nose on the ratty wrist of her sweatshirt. She smiled a smirky smile and nodded at the gallery of admirers. I took her from the living room.

"See?" I said to my friends as I left.

I had planned only two dates with Darla beyond the first one, which had been nothing but sex. One would be to indulge in a crystal meth of a quality I had never encountered, whose granules sparkled an otherworldly lavender, meth that would make all meth I had ever snorted, even the top-ranking stuff bragged to be "glass" by those who sold it, look like yellow crumbles of crank bought off bikers at a truck stop. Darla had been addicted to the stuff in high school—an era that I imagine had only just passed for her, but Darla talked about it like it was a million years ago, sunk deeply in the far-away, her history.

On our other date we would do heroin, something I had never done, had been too smart to do, had learned from the stories of friends who had survived it and was now too old to be experimenting with. It would be inexcusably foolish to try heroin now, at the age of thirty. Heroin was for impressionable, poorly-loved teenagers, or rocker kids in their early twenties pretending it was the '70s. It would be an embarrassment. But as Darla spoke of it, her eyes lush and brown, I realized that always I had wanted to try the drug, just once, and the only reason I hadn't was that I had never been around it. Not in any real sort of way. Homeless addicts shooting up on my doorstep, men trying to sell it to me on my way home, they did not count. It had never been beside me the way Darla was.

So we had our date. Darla rang my doorbell. It was dark outside though early, like 9 or 10, not morning yet, not 3 a.m. It was a real date, not a booty call. Darla had it in her pocket, she'd bought it down the street on her way over. She had a little balloon in her pocket and she hoped, as she tore it open, that she hadn't been ripped off.

She wasn't. The balloon split to reveal twin cellophane baggies twisted slightly together. One held a bit of the worst cocaine ever created. Worse then the stuff we normally purchased at the cocaine bar on Sixteenth Street, from the guy who used to work for the

CIA and who liked to flirt with you in the ladies room as he parceled up your drugs. It was faintly yellow.

"Ugh," Darla shuddered. "You can have it. I wouldn't, though."

Of course I did. It lit me up a little. My light glowed into my bedroom, onto Darla, lit everything right up with me. I smiled. The other bag held a sticky brown pebble.

"Smell it." Darla held it under my nose. The odor was sharp and familiar; it stung my nose. Brown sugar and vinegar.

We snorted dark brown puddles from a spoon. We used tiny straws or the truncated, hollow body of a pen. The pen parts lay cast across my desk, disemboweled like the stolen cars across the street. The cars howled their last howl into the night, electronic and repetitive, then silence. Snorting the drug felt like drowning. It dribbled backwards up into my sinuses. It stung my eyes.

We left the house, walking slowly around the corner to the store on Mission, Fica Market. Drugged-out yahoos clustered around its entrance always, and the clerk was a handsome Middle Eastern kid who was always high as well, his eyes shot through with tiny red veins, bleary, subdued and cheerful. I had read a book about a woman who did heroin all the time. When she did the brown heroin, as opposed to the white powder found on the East Coast, she ate brown foods like chocolate milk and ice cream. I bought a six-pack of Guinness.

"I don't think you'll need that," Darla said. It's true that I was going under, I could feel it there in the garishly lit store, but Darla didn't understand that I always needed it.

I bought it from the guy, we both looked at each other with drooping lids, the skin on our faces heavy. The men out front hooted and slurred. Perhaps my entire neighborhood was wasted. On the walk home I grew shakier, my legs trembled the way they did after me and Darla had sex. My thighs weakened. Darla carried the beer and helped me up the stairs. On my futon I leaned against my wall. It was blank then, dirty white, but soon I would paint it, for Darla, who I would not stop seeing, as she was having a difficult time procuring the lavender speed for our final date.

We would continue to visit with each other, up in my room in the night, until she found it, and she never would. I would paint the wall blue, bright vibrating blue, and hurl fistfuls of sharp silver glitter at the wet paint. They would cling and sparkle there forever and we would be in love, me and Darla. The glitter would run around my futon like an otherworldly river, flashing. It would get in my blankets, stick to our skin. Darla would fuck it into me. It was in our hair, sunk in my thick, dry tangles, sliding on her greasy locks.

Our faces stinging, we would lie back on my futon and let the liquid drugs pool behind our faces, kiss and taste brown sugar and vinegar. The color would drain from my cheeks, I would turn yellow and green. My makeup stood out on the backdrop of my face like Colorforms, pasted there. I would lie still and clammy, breathing oddly, and Darla would fuss around me. Her tolerance of course was stronger. Darla could snort the drug in her car and then go out and do things, go to poetry readings or strip bars or to play videogames. That trip to the market was it for me, I would never leave the house again, high like that. It was too scary, and too embarrassing. I would tilt back on my futon instead. I would feel slow and beautiful like an ailing princess. We pledged to do it only once a week, but we did so little, really, that a single balloon would last us three days. So we would keep it up—three days on, two days off. Me and Darla would ruin each other's lives, but we would fall in love first, in my room above Fourteenth Street.

## Tonight the Muse Is In a Popular Suburban Steakhouse Franchise

**Dan Kennedy**

Connie is recently divorced, has a minor limp from a spontaneous attempt at Rollerblading on a blind date, and works as an accounts payable administrator at a nearby marketing company, and tonight she's teaching me a thing or two about dancing here at the lounge of the Outback Steakhouse in Citrus Heights, California. Showing me how to move anyway I want to the backbeat that The Range is laying down behind Bruce Hornsby. And I'll tell you what, after just having made a cool three hundred bucks for a recent contribution to *Reader's Digest*, I'm having no problem feeling every word of Bruce's lyric when he sings "that's just the way it is." I'm a writer on my way to the top tonight, and that's just the way it is. Connie can tell. She can kind of feel that there's something about me being here tonight, but she has no idea that I was published into the October issue of the *Digest*. Frankly, it's just as well that she knows nothing about it. Especially since she works in Accounts Payable, and the joke I had contributed to the 'All In a Day's Work' section just happened to be a joke about an accounts payable administrator who forgets to pay an invoice sent in by a vendor. In my joke, when the character is asked by her supervisor why the vendor hasn't been paid, she replies that the vendor just happens to be her ex-husband. When the boss is scratching his head still trying to figure out what that has to do with anything, she makes a crack about this particular vendor being late with an alimony payment, and explains that she has simply taken the amount owed to him and paid herself. Then right at the point in the joke where you think she'll be reprimanded for this, the boss actually applauds her for having "cut out the middleman" and gives her a big raise. So there's really nothing bad about the accounts payable character in my joke. I mean, she's smart, effective, and even ends up winning in the end but I just feel better dancing the night away with Connie without her knowing about my writing. Without her worrying if my next *Digest* piece will be about an accounts payable administrator with a slight limp and a penchant for Long Island ice teas at the Outback Steakhouse.

These are heady days. Something happened when I saw the tiny five-point italicized type that spelled my name at the end of my submission just before the phrase, 'submitted by email.' I can honestly say that's when things changed for me. That's the moment I knew that I would no longer be a nervous misfit who never seemed to meet women. It's also when I knew that family and friends would start to ask favors of me on account of my *Reader's Digest* connections. They would start trying out material on me in conversations. We would be talking about anything from a favorite restaurant to the weather when they would suddenly say, "Hey, speaking of laughter being the best medicine, don't you think it would be funny if a clergyman and the owner of a local grocery store, blah, blah, blah, blah, blah."

I would trail off and stop paying attention. To the joke, and to the heartbreak that came with knowing friends were using me to open doors at the *Digest.* My ex-girlfriend Kristin even had the nerve to pitch me something that she thought would be a perfect fit for the 'Real Life Drama' section in the June issue. She said, "It's a 'Turning Point' piece about a young woman who risks a life of loneliness and sadness by breaking up with her struggling writer boyfriend, only to end up happier than ever when she meets a new guy who has a real job and some financial stability."

But I'm not going to stand here on the dance floor tonight and complain about what's happened for me since my 'All In a Day's Work' piece was published. Because there are plenty of plusses to having a workplace-related short humor item published in the magazine that the mostly divorced 48-to-63-year-old female demographic holds dear. Plusses like standing here on the dance floor knowing for the first time in my life that there would be women to meet in any chain steakhouse that I set foot in on my travels.

The Contemporary Rock compilation CD that the Outback management is playing tonight has shifted gears into something a little more up-tempo. And Connie isn't about to let me leave the dance floor. She goes right into this thing you've seen before where the woman kind of lowers her shoulders in a forward slump and starts wagging them toward the floor one at a time. Wag the right shoulder down and the left one up, and vice versa, pull the chin in and peer playfully fierce at the man you're dancing with. Two more Meyer's Rum Screaming Coconut Teazers and I was going to wind up someplace I shouldn't be winding up tonight.

The whole point of my Central California travels was to be finding the inspiration to think up my next piece to submit, and after only four magical nocturnal explorations of Stockton, Hayward, West Sacramento, and now Citrus Heights, California, I was making my research way more about pleasure than work. It happens to every writer. You're free of distraction and able to focus when you're nobody, but get a little taste of that $300 check after your joke gets picked up and suddenly you're traveling to explore semi-upscale steakhouse franchises and party with anybody who's in the mood to push the envelope. All in hopes of luring the muse into the shadow of nightfall and writing just one more piece as good as that one that started it all for you.

When Connie finally gave me a break from the dancing, we made our way up to the bar to cool down. She ordered a glass full of ice water. The bartender told her he didn't have a fly swatter.

The music was pretty loud, so Connie raised her voice and clarified that she had said, "...glass full of ice Water. NOT FLY SWATTER."

Everybody within earshot started laughing. Except me. I was furiously scribbling notes of the comedic misunderstanding onto cocktail napkins. I had just found my next submission. A little something about Life in these United States.

# A Case Study of Emergency Room Procedure and Risk-Management by Hospital Staff Members in the Urban Facility

Stacey Richter

I.

Subject 525, a Caucasian female in her early to mid-twenties, entered an emergency medical facility at around 11 p.m. presenting symptoms of an acute psychotic episode. Paranoia, heightened sensitivity to physical contact, and high volume vocal emanations were noted at triage by the medical staff. The subject complained of the hearing of voices, specifically "a choir of amphibians" who were entreating the subject to "pretty please guard the product from the evil frog prince." The staff reported that the subject's bizarre behavior was augmented by an unusual sartorial style, commenting that she was "an ethereal young woman wearing a Renaissance-type dress, with huge knots in her long, otherwise flowing hair." She was accompanied by a strange odor, tentatively identified as "cat urine."

During the intake interview, the subject volunteered the information that she had nasally inhaled "crystal," estimating that she had nasally inhaled (snorted) between 50 and 250 mg of "crystal" in the twenty-four hours prior to hospital admission. "Crystal," it was determined, is a slang term for methamphetamine, a central nervous system stimulant similar to prescription amphetamines such as Benzedrine. Methamphetamine is a "street" drug-of-abuse that has become popular in recent years due to its easy manufacture possibilities (Osborne, 1988). It sometimes referred to by the terms crystal, speed, zoomazoom, and go fast (Durken, 1972). In a brief moment of lucidity, Subject 525 theorized that her psychotic state might be due to the large quantity of methamphetamine she had "snorted," and the staff agreed to put her in a "nice, quiet, white room" for a period of observation. The head resident thought it advisable to administer antipsychotic medication, but the subject, who by all accounts exhibited an uncanny amount of personal charm, prevailed upon the staff to give her a can of beer instead.

II.

After approximately sixty minutes of observation, a member of the nursing staff noted that the subject had begun to complain that "a be-slimed prince" was causing certain problems for her, namely "using copper fittings" and "not ventilating right." This "prince" was, as the nurse understood it, acting "all mean and horrible" concerning the manufacture of methamphetamine, which the subject had cheerfully volunteered as her occupation during the intake interview. The nurse, who was formerly employed in a Federal prison and had considerable experience treating denizens of the demimonde, theorized that "Prince" might by a moniker used by the subject's "old man"; this was particularly likely, the nurse indicated, since the manufacture of methamphetamine is the customary province of "gangs" of motorcycle riders, who often use colorful nicknames as a way of asserting their "outsider" status in society (Ethel Kreztchner, R.N., 2002).

The nurse further asserted that this would explain why the subject had offered, at intake, only the name "Princess," and would indicate no surname. By then the hour had grown rather late, and as the emergency room was quiet, much of the staff gathered around the subject ("Princess") who began to tell a lively tale of capture and imprisonment by a handsome but wicked "prince" who was, in fact, "an evil enchanter." The tradition of shape-shifting sorcerers is a familiar one in old German folk tales (Grimm, ca. 1812), though these tales have been widely regarded as fanciful narratives concocted to intimidate and control unruly juveniles (twelve and under) in diverse cultural contexts, and are rarely considered historical evidence. Nevertheless, the Princess claimed that the Prince had captured her from an orphanage near Eloy, Arizona, where she had spent her days climbing trees in pursuit of nuts. Chasing butterflies, according to the subject, was another activity she enjoyed in her youth. But that all changed when a handsome young man approached the girl and offered her a pony made of candy. The pony was beautiful and delicious, and though the Princess wished to save it forever, she found she devoured it anyway. With every bite the pony grew smaller. And with every bite the handsome "young man" become more fearsome and wicked looking.

The staff gathered close, listening with great interest. The Princess went on to indicate that the Prince/Sorcerer had bewitched her with the candy horse, and had since imprisoned her in a pre-fabricated "home" near a foul-smelling landfill, where she was kept locked up in a "tin can with carpet taped over the windows." There, the Prince had prevailed upon her to undertake the smelly and dangerous manufacture of methamphetamine by means of his sorcerer's power. All day long, the Princess said, she was forced to "boil down Mexican ephedrine in a triple-neck flask, bubble hydrogen through a stainless steel tank, or titrate ethyl ether out of lock defrosting fluid, dressed only filthy rags," while the Prince rode his shiny "hog" through tall pines in the mountains to the north of town. Or the Prince would "relax and kick back with a can of brew" while the Princess "slaved over a hot chemistry set." The only positive aspect of the experience, the Princess noted, was that she "cooked the best damn product in Arizona," a substance that was uncommonly potent and white, she said, with a "real clean buzz."

The Princess explained, in a sweetly chiming voice, that these endeavors were dangerous, particularly under the conditions imposed by the Prince, who habitually smoked marijuana cigarettes in the vicinity of fumes. She had survived because she was protected by a special angel, one with "gills" who could exist underwater or possibly "inside a solution." She referred to this angel as "Gilbert," (possibly "Gillbert") and noted that Gilbert appeared to her when she imbibed heavily of "the product." The manifestation of angels, seraphim, djinns and Elvis Presley is common during episodes of psychosis (Hotchkiss, 1969), and much of the staff believed that the Princess was describing an aspect of methamphetamine-induced hallucination. Others on staff found themselves strangely moved by the Princess's story of forced enslavement and the high-risk game of organic chemistry, and wondered if there might be some sort of truth to it.

The head resident, in particular, took an interest in the subject's case, indicating to researchers that he was "bored that night, as usual" and that he found the Princess "interesting." The resident further indicated that his prodigious academic success was based on his above-average intelligence, which was also "a curse" because it led him to feel a feeling of "boredom," and intolerance with all of "the idiots around him," which, he made clear, also applied to the researchers gathering data on this case. Researchers in turn described the resident as rather "vain and haughty," or "arrogant," though most theorized that these traits covered up insecurity about his youth combined with a doomed romanticism undercut by a persistent tendency toward bitterness.

The Princess was exhibiting fewer symptoms of psychosis, and had become quite comfortable in her surroundings, curling up in a nest of pillows "like a cat" (Overhand, 2002). She said that she loved the medical staff and was grateful to them for helping to save her from the evilness of the Prince and the pungent squalidness of methamphetamine manufacture. The head resident shuffled his feet and pointed out that the Princess herself had actually contributed to her own care by wisely seeking medical treatment when she felt overwhelmed by drug-induced psychosis, whereas a lot of "tweaked-out idiots" just went ahead and did something stupid or violent. Then the two stared for a while into each other's eyes.

It was then that lateness of the hour was nervously remarked upon by all, and several staff members complained that they had been on duty for an excessive length of time. The Princess made a "general comment" that her product could "give a person a little pick-me-up" that theoretically might make the staff members feel like "they were operating at one hundred and fifty percent."

The staff was curious about the efficacy of the Princess's homemade methamphetamine, though their enthusiasm abated somewhat after a phlebotomist (a "pretty plump girl who never wore any makeup and never smiled or said hello to nobody beneath her," according to the environmental control officer) recited aloud in a high and quavering voice a list of the possible effects of nasally inhaling methamphetamine, including "nervousness, sweating, teeth-gnashing, irritability, incessant talking, sleeplessness, and the obsessive assembling and disassembling of machinery" (PDR, 2002). Interest swelled once again when the Princess pointed out that the young phlebotomist had mumbled while mentioning one of the chief effects of the substance: euphoria.

After that, the staff cleared from the small room where the Princess was being kept sequestered by herself, though occasionally a lone member would disappear inside, to emerge a few moments later wiping their nose with eyes unusually wild. Such staff members were also observed tidying their work areas, peering into the mirror, smoking cigarettes, and talking to one another with great animation and enthusiasm but little content (Overhand, 2002). The receptionist was observed taking apart a telephone, so that she could "clean it." The overall effect was that the staff was unusually energetic and "happy" (see below).

III.

Shortly before dawn, several nurses returned to the Princess's bedside, where they adjusted the lighting in the small room so a warm glow bathed the subject. They worked with combs to untangle the knots in the subject's hair. The head resident had entered the room as well, and kept his boyish face, so incongruous beneath his balding head, hunched toward his chest while he made notes in the subject's chart.

It was then that the subject began to speak softly about a set of ponies she had made out of old tires. The Princess explained how she had "freed" the ponies from the rubber with a cutting implement, and that a "herd" of such ponies hung from ropes in the trees around her prefabricated housing unit, where they blew back and forth in the breeze, bumping against each other with hollow thuds. They possessed the spirit of "running things," she explained, though they had no "legs to speak of," she could look at them and feel the feeling of "something wild and running away." The subject further explained that nasally inhaling or "skin popping" (subcutaneous injection) of methamphetamine gave her relief from a feeling that "nothing important would ever happen to her," and replaced it with the sensation that she was, like the ponies fashioned from discarded tires, something "wild and running away."

She indicated that these feelings of flight accounted for the only times that she ever truly felt like a princess.

IV.

The notes in the subject's chart at this point become "tiny and very, very neat," according to researchers (Plank et al., 2002). The notes themselves indicate that the subject was "an exceptionally attractive woman," and that the medical staff found her "enchanting." She was "like them but different—more perfect—yet at the same time more glassine and fragile." The chart noted that the subject had become sleepy, perhaps due to the fatigue that often follows the ingestion of methamphetamine (Nintzel, 1982). It was indicated that some members of the staff wished to allow her to sleep, while others had an urgent need to "pester her; to poke her in the leg with a stick over and over," to keep her awake.

Verbal accounts indicate that not all the members of the night staff were equally smitten with the subject. Several members demurred, in particular the phlebotomist, who commented that the subject was "a disgusting drug addict" who was "manipulative." She added that she hated men "who fall for those poor lost creatures," even though such "creatures" were in the process of getting "exactly what they signed up for." The phlebotomist indicated that it was futile to try to help the subject, save medically, because the subject had freely chosen her own seedy destiny, despite her weird story of kidnapping, adding that "not everybody who suffers has a burning need to dramatize it with scarves and eyeliner."

V.

Videotapes from the security cameras in the waiting area provide a clear visual record of the intrusion that occurred at approximately 4:12 a.m. The tapes show a clean, tiled area violently rent by the shiny chrome form of a very large motorcycle (or "hog") piloted by the "Prince," who gained ingress by method of riding through the glass doors, where he continued to gun his motorcycle in circles through a reception area furnished with chairs which became smashed. The "Prince" was reported to be a large, muscular male of indeterminate race sporting "a pair of sideburns as big as teacups." He was reportedly clad in "enough black leather to denude several cows," though naturally it has not been determined how many cows would have been needed to provide the amount of leather the Prince was wearing. Much of the hospital staff on duty also reported that the intruder had a "tail, slimy and black, sort of like the tail of a tadpole." Careful scrutiny of security videotapes does reveal the presence of a whiplike appendage dangling from the back of the Prince's "hog," though the possibility that this might in fact be a literal "tail" has been discounted by researchers, who have chalked up this and several other aspects of the medical staff's report to group suggestibility (Ostreicher, 2002). (For example, the hospital staff also reported that the Prince had "eyes that glowed red like coals" and that "lizards and snakes slithered from his boots.")

It was reported that the Prince then parked his "hog" and proceeded past the reception area, stalking the warren-like halls of the emergency treatment facility in his heavy boots, scuffing the floor, screaming that someone had taken his "woman," and wondering aloud, in a yelling tone, where he could find his "kitten."

At this the Princess and hospital staff fled to a supply closet, where they cowered, leaving the issue of how to properly control the "Prince" unresolved. It was agreed that the police, as well as the hospital security guards, should be alerted; it was lamented however that there was no available phone in the supply closet and such action would require someone to dash out into the hallway where the Prince was raging and overturning carts and smashing his hammer-like hands into walls while eating candy reserved for children who were unfortunate enough to wind up in the emergency room. The Princess, whose melodic voice was muffled due to the press of bodies in the supply closet, pointed out that the Prince possessed special evil magic powers and that anyone who challenged him must be good in heart and clever both, and carry with him or her a small silver bell which the Princess kept on a chain around her neck.

As the destructive noises of the Prince's rampage became louder, the head resident indicated that he felt he should be the one to make an effort to save himself, the staff, and the once-psychotic but now quite sweet Princess. The staff was surprised to hear this, as they had never noticed any behavior related to bravery or even simple kindness on the part of the head resident. They continued to be surprised when they heard him say, in a quavering voice, that though it was true he might not be good-hearted, he certainly was clever enough, so why not give it a go? Everyone in the closet gave him a quiet but heartfelt round of applause. The Princess begged him to be careful and hung the bell around his neck with a trembling hand. She bestowed upon him a soft kiss as he slipped out the door.

The "rescue" of women by handsome, effeminate men is a staple of old folktales, engineered to reconcile a young woman's inclinations towards feckless independence with the prevailing custom of marriage by casting the potential husband as really nice and sort of harmless and at the very least a whole lot better than the alternative of living with her dysfunctional family (cf. Cinderella, Grimm, 1812). Despite the tradition of the effeminate male triumphing over the more sexual, "animal" challenger, it seemed uncertain to all present that the head resident could defeat the "Prince" using the tools at his disposal: a stethoscope, some pens, and a pager. It's difficult to determine, though, what kind of damage the resident may have been capable of inflicting with these devices since, according to his own account, when confronted with the fierce and gruesome "Prince" who "smelled like burning rubber and had white stuff hanging off his beard," he froze then mutely raised a traitorous arm to point to the supply closet where the Princess and the rest of the staff were hiding.

The Prince wrenched open the door with a huge paw, and out popped the Princess.

According to the staff, the Princess screamed with a high-pitched yelp when the Prince grabbed her, smearing her lovely Renaissance-style dress with grease. The records note that the Prince and the Princess together presented quite an odd picture, one that brought to mind "a nightmare creature clawing a plate of a petit fours" (Petix, 2002). The Princess is reported to have said, "It's okay," and, "No, but I want to go with him, really," and, "He's my old man!" in a tone of tense brightness, but the staff plainly did not believe her and theorized that she was simply trying to "appease her oppressor" in order to minimize the likelihood of domestic violence. Before the staff was able to contact the authorities, the "Prince" settled himself astride his hog and pulled the Princess up behind him.

The Prince and Princess roared out of the building and vanished into the night in a cloud of exhaust.

## Conclusion

After the Prince and Princess had departed, the staff grumbled that the head resident had behaved "most cowardly," and complained that the Princess had been "sacrificed," to be "whisked off to a prefabricated house where everything is always fast and tinged with madness, or else dark and sad and falling asleep." Much of the staff argued that something should have been done to help the girl, though some felt it was the curse of the phylum Princess to be always at the mercy of one prince-type or another, and that her best chance was to save herself, which seemed unlikely. The resident, for his part, quickly aligned himself with the phlebotomist, agreeing that the Princess was "just an addict" who had come in "exhibiting drug-seeking behavior anyway," and implying, in word and action, that drug addicts were by nature less than human and so deserved whatever nasty fate they got. Then he skulked off down a fluorescent-lit hallway with his hands shoved into his pockets.

Though he wore the silver bell around his neck to the end of his days.

## The Right Way to Eat a Bagel

### Marshall Moore

A gust of cold early-March air buffeted George, distracting him from his crossword puzzle. He looked up to see if Angela had arrived. She'd said to expect a short black woman with shoulder-length braids and a brown leather jacket, glasses, but not wearing make-up, no way, not this time of night. The diner door swung shut behind a chunky young white guy with acne. George turned his attention back to his half-empty pint of Guinness and the smudged newsprint on the table in front of him.

George hated crossword puzzles and wouldn't have been working this one if he hadn't been in a hurry to get out of his apartment. Meeting Angela like this, in the middle of the night, had to be the most impulsive thing he'd done in recent memory. On the other hand, why not? It had been her idea, and what exactly did he have to lose? He was desperate for a change of scene, some fresh air, a different perspective. A conversation with someone who had no vested interest in talking him into anything or out of it, either. He'd been a little stir-crazy, and not quite ready to close his eyes. Now here he was. A previous someone had left a disheveled copy of today's *Post* on the table; George had read the articles that interested him while draining his first pint, waiting. That left him two choices: staring out the window like a lost soul in an Edward Hopper painting, or attempting the crossword puzzle.

Why did the puzzles he worked call for words like 'ennui' and 'narthex' and 'cedilla'? Case in point: this one featured celebrity trivia. George knew a bit about literature and film, yes, but he tuned out the gossipy media as much as possible. Especially now, during Oscar season. Off the top of his head, he could name the actor who had played the reporter in Fellini's *8 1/2*, but could he name the seven-figure hunk who had played opposite Nicole Kidman in her last two films, and was there a reason why he should care?

The waitress stopped by.

"You want some chips or fries or a sandwich or somethin'?"

George shook his head.

"Just another one of these when I'm done," he said. "And a crossword puzzle dictionary, if you've got one."

"Oh sure, no problem," the waitress, a cute but Q-tip skinny redhead named Elyce, said through her mouthful of gum. Her cinnamon-scented breath seemed to cling to him. "We keep two or three around for customers. They're by the cash register. I'll bring one right over."

"You're kidding," George said.

"Of course I am. This is a diner. I'll bring you some chips, though. You look like you could use a bowl of chips."

George shrugged. He clicked his fingernails on the tabletop, which was smeary from the moist bits of food and beverage splashes Elyce had no doubt been wiping away all day with an increasingly grimy hand towel: pale gray streaks over pink Formica gloss.

"I'm waiting for someone," he said.

"Who isn't?"

Elyce the waitress walked away and George studied the white squares on the crossword puzzle again, waiting for either Angela or some flash of verbal insight to arrive like a deus ex machina in an ancient Greek tragedy.

. . .

*George:* i don't really understand why you're online... you know, in a chat room. you don't sound like someone who does this all the time.

*Angela:* I'm not, this is my first time, my husband is away on business and I just turned on the computer and here I am

*George:* had to talk to someone? had to make a connection?=)

*Angela:* I'm not sure what I'm looking for, just to talk with somebody I suppose. What's that thing you did, with the equals sign?

*George:* this? =)? look at it sideways, it's a smiley face. see?

*Angela:* That's cute. You're cute. Thank you.

. . .

This is a bad idea. This whole thing has BAD IDEA written all over it in big red letters. I should pay for my beer and go home and just forget about Angela.

George's grip on the base of his beer mug would have strangled the glass if it had been alive. He twitched, from nerves he guessed, and his hand slipped on condensation. The glass pitched to one side and sloshed Guinness across the crossword puzzle. Affleck hometown (Boston, number 29 Across) and Fred and (Ginger, number 18 Down) and the empty stack of squares where Nicole Kidman's hot new romantic lead should have gone were all reduced to a Rorschach blotch of carbonated, alcoholic ink.

This did not make George entirely unhappy.

At least now I don't have to finish filling the goddamn thing out, not with two-thirds of it soaked.

Another burst of cold air signalled the arrival of someone new, and when George looked up from the soggy mess of newspaper in front of him, he knew he'd lost his chance to slip away. A guilty blush warmed his face as Angela closed the distance between the door and his booth.

When she slid onto the bench opposite and extended a hand to shake, George's first thought was, She's prettier than I expected.

George classified female attractiveness along three axes: Pretty, Cute, and Hot. Pretty women were the even-featured ones who had been the girls next door growing up, the ones his mother wanted him to take out on dates and marry and impregnate. They had clear skin and symmetrical faces and an air of steadiness about them. Cute women tended to be the shorter ones who seemed younger than they perhaps really were. The facial topology could be more varied but they smiled a lot and were easy to like. And the Hot women, well, they were the ones who smoldered like runway models with no panties on under their Prada. He would expect a Hot woman to snarl, "Say my name, bitch!" in bed but not a Pretty one, for example.

Julia, George's ex-wife, had been a stunning amalgam of all three. She still was, he assumed. And she was gone now, wasn't she? George refused to let himself dwell on her. Enough damage had already been done.

And Angela? Pretty, yes, actually, somewhat to his surprise. Not for the first time, George suspected his rating system fell short when he tried to use it on non-white women. Black women, for example, could be Regal in a way that no white woman ever could. The towering cheekbones and the imperious bearing gave these women an air of being mistresses of all they surveyed.

This was probably the worst idea of my life, agreeing to come out on a night like this, tonight of all nights. She's going to think I'm a loser. By any objective standard, she wouldn't be wrong.

"Firm handshake," George said.

"I'm in upper management," Angela said. "I didn't get there by batting my eyelashes at people."

"Break many bones with that grip?"

"More balls than bones," Angela said. "Is the coffee here any good or should I just order a beer?"

"I guess it depends on the outcome you want," George said. "Caffeine or alcohol. Do you want to wake up or go to sleep?"

"Yes," Angela said.

This took George a second. "Right," he said. "Yes. That would be why we're here."

Angela stared at him. "I know why I'm here," she said. She turned and looked around for the waitress, apparently saw her, raised her eyebrows, and nodded in a Come-over-here way. "Are you sure you do?"

A darkness smiled in the center of George, and he filled it with his remaining two inches of Guinness.

"I don't want you to talk me into or out of anything," he said. He wiped his mouth with the back of his hand. "I'm clear on that much."

"Oh you sounded pretty clear on what you wanted," Angela said. "I guess that's the real reason I'm here."

"You wanted to see my clarity for yourself?"

"You could say that."

"First time anyone's ever wanted me for my clarity," George said.

Elyce returned to take their orders, two beers and a basket of fries to supplement the stale chips George hadn't touched, and left an oily kitchen smell lingering in her wake. George knew he and Angela would leave this diner reeking of grease. Soon enough, they'd bundle up in their coats and leave, with the waxy stink of the griddle in their hair, their clothes, their pores. Despite the cold temperature and the blustery wind, their noses would still pick up the odor. In the grand scheme of things, he supposed it mattered very little. George had other things on his mind, and Angela could go back to her family and her life smelling like an artery-hardening midnight snack.

Number Eighteen Across: lox. George hadn't filled that one in (smoked and orange) but an idle glance down at the dry half of the crossword brought the word to mind.

"What am I supposed to talk to you about, then?" asked Angela after a silence.

Their beers came.

"We should talk about normal things," George said. "Tell me the right way to eat a bagel. Do you toast yours and coat them with cream cheese? Do you like lox?"

"You're nervous," Angela said. "I don't think you're committed to seeing this through."

George knew his hands were shaking, and he couldn't warm up no matter how much beer he poured down his throat.

"I've come this far," he said, meeting her gaze.

She studied him a moment, then sipped her beer.

"I'm probably old enough to be your mother," Angela said.

"Don't say that," George said. "That's impossible."

Angela smiled and took another sip. Someone fed the jukebox, and an old Pink Floyd dirge filled the diner: *Set the controls for the heart of the sun…*

"Okay, I won't say that. Maybe it's true and maybe it's not. Maybe I'm trying to shake you up a little. Is that such a bad thing?"

"I'm nervous." George looked down.

Angela reached across the table and took his hand.

"I hate lox," she said. "But garlic bagels are a weakness of mine. Lots of cream cheese. The kind with chives in it. We're going to be just fine, okay?"

. . .

*Angela:* I've never done this before. Is it OK for me to ask what you look like?

*George:* that's fine, you can ask me whatever you want

*Angela:* Oh no, anything? I don't think I want to go that far... besides, if you sent me a picture I wouldn't know what to do with it.

*George:* it's kind of funny

*Angela:* What's funny about it?

*George:* my expectations, maybe. i just didn't have this in mind when i signed on

*Angela:* So are you going to tell me what you look like? I want to know who I'm talking to.

*George:* late 20s. red hair. freckles. kind of handsome i guess, depending on what you're into

*Angela:* You know I'm married, don't you? With kids. And I'm an African American.

*George:* great, good, cool. i had a wife once, for a few minutes.

*Angela:* What happened?

*George:* i'm still trying to figure that out but i guess it doesn't matter anymore, she's still gone

. . .

"You loved your wife very much," Angela said, releasing George's hand.

"What makes you say that?"

"That lost look on your face. I think that's the real reason you wanted me to meet you here. I've been married a long time. Maybe you wanted my perspective as much as I wanted yours."

"Are you sure that's what this is about? Perspective?"

Angela nodded.

"All right then. Yes. I loved her."

"And that's why you're doing this?"

"No. I mean, maybe that's part of it, but there's so much..." George stopped to think. "It's not for just one reason. So my business failed and I'm bankrupt and my wife left me. For a woman, if you want to know."

Angela nodded again and sipped more beer. "Another woman. How about that. That's happened in my family, too. Is she happier now?"

"She hasn't called to let me know. I'd like to know. I have to hope she is, after what she put me through."

"And where do I come in?" Angela asked.

"The door over there?" George smiled. "I think that's where you came in. Although I might have been hallucinating."

"Grief'll do that to you."

"I just want to feel better," George said. "I mean, I haven't been expecting to be on top of the world, but better? It's not unreasonable. It keeps not happening."

"You're trying to talk yourself out of it," Angela said softly. "Would it make you feel any better if I said I understood?"

"How could you?"

"I have a husband and great kids and a nice home, so my life must be perfect," Angela said. "That's why I came out on a night like this. Didn't it occur to you to ask where my kids were?"

George had to admit the thought had never crossed his mind. He had wanted to start a family with Julia. Once upon a time. Perhaps this proved he had never been cut out for paternity, that he didn't think to ask about her kids straight away. Did that indicate some deficit in his priorities, some inherent unsuitability? Or were kids something you had to get used to? If it was such a complicated thing, having a family, why did so many people do it? And how?

"With their aunt. Who would have me locked up if she knew I was out in the middle of the night like this. With a white guy at least fifteen years younger than me." She smiled at him as if she'd made a very small joke.

"So your life is not perfect," George said. "Forgive me for assuming it was."

"It's not perfect," Angela whispered.

They looked at each other. Elyce broke the spell by asking if they were okay, did they need anything else, some coffee, a sandwich, some chicken nuggets? More chips?

Strychnine, George thought. Something very old-fashioned like that. Arsenic.

"We're just great, honey," Angela said.

She turned her head to watch Elyce walked away.

"How do you want to do it?" Angela asked.

"What?"

"You know what I mean. I want you to tell me what you have in mind."

George opened his mouth and closed it. A sourness crept up the back of his throat.

"You really want me to tell you. Right now. You actually want me to describe it."

"Yes," Angela said. "I do."

"What if I just wanted you to have a normal conversation with me?" George asked. This felt like treading water in a whirlpool: dark currents dragged him down. His palms filmed, and he wiped them against his jeans. The stickiness lingered.

"I already told you how I like my bagels."

"What's your husband's name? Your kids? How old are they? What grades are they in?"

Angela shook her head. "I don't know what to say."

"You don't know the names of your husband and kids?"

"Of course I do. But this is the last conversation you're ever going to have with another living human being, and you want to talk about bagels and my kids?"

"Yes. No. I don't know," George said. He drained his glass. Might as well optimize his alcohol intake. Look at it as getting things underway.

"Tell me how you're going to do it."

"I can't."

"You're not going to go through with it, then?" Angela asked. "You're going to lose your nerve?"

George shook his head. Tears stung the corners of his eyes.

"I just wanted to talk to someone," he said. "Someone *real.* Julia's gone. My family... I can't do that to them, call in the middle of the night like this, knowing what it'll be like for them afterward."

Angela took a deep breath. "Maybe I came here to meet you for inspiration," she said.

"Maybe I'm braver than I knew."

"What do you mean?"

"There's a reason I asked how you were going to do it," she said.

"What do you mean?" George asked. Then it hit him. "Oh. You?"

She nodded. She started to speak and seemed to get choked up, as if there were a word she couldn't force out of her mouth. She grabbed the pen and wrote something in the dry corner of the crossword puzzle, a terrible word that when he saw it, didn't fit with any of the clues he'd been given so far: CANCER.

. . .

*Angela:* So why is it such a surprise, you're talking to me?

*George:* i guess this makes it real

*Angela:* Makes what real?

*George:* last night on earth

*Angela:* I'm sorry?

*Angela:* Hello? Are you there?

*Angela:* George? Hey, be nice to me, I'm new at this, remember?

*George:* never mind, i'm being cryptic. i shouldn't have dragged you into this

*George:* look, this is the last conversation i'll ever have with anyone, as far as i know

*Angela:* Because?

*George:* think about it

*George:* you haven't typed anything for a few minutes, does that mean you're thinking?

*Angela:* I think I've figured it out. But why?

*George:* i should leave you alone. you have your own life. you don't need this

*Angela:* Well, now that you've done it, you can't back out now... We ought to talk.

. . .

"I got the idea from an old girlfriend," George said. He surveyed the beer left in his glass. "I've nicknamed it 'combo therapy'. I bought a tank of carbon dioxide from a science supply store. When I get home, I'm going to seal up my bathroom to make it airtight, duct tape around the doorframe, and then I'm going to drink and take pills until I pass out. I won't wake up."

"Very elaborate," Angela said.

"How are you guys doing?" Elyce asked, from out of nowhere.

George jumped. Nerves, he supposed.

"Fine," Angela said.

"Another beer," George spoke up a bit as Elyce turned away. Then, to Angela, he asked, "You're going to?"

She looked down. Nodded.

"My church teaches that it's a sin. But what's right about putting my family through hell? There's no treatment for... what I have. The bills will ruin them. How is that the right thing to do?" Her voice hitched at the end. "Both choices are terrifying."

"I envy you in a way," George said.

Angela looked up sharply. "Why is that?"

"You have a family. You have the comfort of a church. Religion. I'm kind of flying solo here."

"That's one way of looking at it," Angela said. "I'm not sure if that makes me feel better, but it's something to think about."

"I completely underestimated you," George said. A truck rumbled past, rattling the windows. He looked back at Angela.

"It wouldn't be the first time I've been underestimated," she said.

Were there bags under her eyes or was it the light? George scrutinized her face for signs of illness. How impolite would it be to ask what kind of cancer she had, where it was, why it couldn't be treated? Was she in pain? Could she feel the diseased cells crowding out the healthy ones? Weren't they kind of off the edge of the world now, where most rules and conventions no longer applied? Of course he could ask those questions, he concluded after a moment's thought. Those and many others. The thing was, did he really want to know? He'd come here to have a conversation about nothing, after all, before going home to his pills and his gas tank.

"I read about a medieval form of torture," Angela said. "The victim would be immobilized, tied to a chair or something. A rat would be put in a metal urn, with the mouth of the urn against the victim's belly. They'd heat up the urn until the rat freaked out. It would be so desperate to escape it would burrow into the only soft surface it could find..."

"Oh God, stop," George said. His gorge rose.

"Cancer took my mother," Angela said. "It seems to run in our family, this particular kind. I know what I'm in for, and it's a lot like what I just described to you. I'm..." She trailed off, shaking her head. "I'm not going through that. I'm not going to do that to my husband and my kids."

George stared out the window again. He couldn't meet her gaze. The corners of his eyes stung. Outside, the corona of mist around the streetlight was the color of a candle about to gutter out. A truck rumbled by.

"I have no idea what to say," George said. "This almost makes me feel selfish. Petty."

"Maybe you don't have to say a word," Angela said.

"I don't have cancer."

"I didn't come here to talk you out of it," she said. "Nobody holds the exclusive rights to pain. It's not an absolute. You make your choices."

"But..."

Angela looked away from him and shrugged her shoulders. A certain tension seemed to leave her face, a certain heaviness. George couldn't be sure. She underwent some subtle shift, as if she'd made a decision, satisfied herself somehow. He looked around the diner: two college students in sparkly clubwear were staring into mugs of coffee; several men around a table by the door were having a loud conversation with their mouths full; one girl who looked too young to be out at this time of night was eating a sandwich and picking her nose as if she were alone—a bruise purpled one side of her face.

"Maybe we've said everything we need to say to each other," Angela said.

She stood abruptly, murmured something that sounded like 'Goodnight', and strode toward the door. For a second or two, George watched her walk away, her braids bouncing, without the reality of her departure sinking in.

"Wait a minute," he said.

But Angela was already out of earshot.

"Wait a minute!"

Heads turned. The bruised girl withdrew the finger from her nose and stared at her nail as if she'd extracted a diamond instead of a moist crust of snot. The raucous discussion by the door stopped. George jumped to his feet, dashed across the diner, skidded in the slippery place by the front door.

"Hey!"

He recognized Elyce's voice, calling after him.

"Just a minute," he said to her, flinging the door open.

Without his coat, the wind was a cold polar bear slap across the face. It had claws. A gust of wet rain stung his cheeks and forehead. His clothes were instantly soaked.

"Angela!"

She stood on the curb with her face in her hands, as if oblivious to the weather. Her shoulders were hunched up. She seemed to be crying.

"Angela!"

And, a second too late, he saw what she was about to do. 'I didn't come here to talk you out of anything,' Angela had said. She stepped off the curb.

The words reverberated in George's head as a horn blared and screams erupted through the night. With a screech of brakes and a horrific thud, Angela disappeared beneath a speeding pickup truck. He had a split-second image of her body being dragged, of a tire crossing her chest, sinking into her as if it were no more substantial than a heap of newspaper, and then both the truck and the night were still.

'Maybe I'm trying to shake you up a little,' Angela had said. 'Maybe I came here to meet you for inspiration.' Both choices are terrifying.

George ignored the screams and the cries of "Sir!"—he recognized the voice as Elyce's in some dim and unconcerned region of his brain—and set off at a brisk walk down the street in the direction of his apartment. He hunched forward to keep the drizzle out of his face.

Only a few hours left until sunrise. Better not to think about this too much.

'Maybe I'm stronger than I knew,' Angela had said.

"Maybe so, maybe not," George said to himself, mostly to drown out the terrible soundtrack in his head: truck colliding with body, horns, screams. He took a deep breath, thrust his hands into his pockets, and walked a little faster.

Don't think about it, George, he ordered himself. Just go home and do it.

## Contributor Notes

JONATHAN AMES (Everybody Dies in Memphis) is the author of *I Pass Like Night, The Extra Man, What's Not to Love?, My Less Than Secret Life*, and *Wake Up, Sir!*.

TODD PRUZAN (No Fear) is an editor at *Print*. He's the co-author (with a 19th-century children's writer) of *The Clumsiest People in Europe* (Bloomsbury USA). He lives in Brooklyn.

RICK MOODY'S (Automatic) celebrated books include three novels and two collections of short fiction. He is a past recipient of the Addison Metcalf Award and a Guggenheim Fellowship. His fiction and essays have appeared in many major publications. He lives in New York.

RICHARD RUSHFIELD (Stalker's Paradise) lives in Los Angeles and is an editor at *Vanity Fair*. He is the author of *On Spec*.

ELIZABETH ELLEN'S (Listen) stories can be found in or on *McSweeney's, Pindeldyboz, Monkeybicycle, Hobart* and *The Guardian*. Currently she resides in Ann Arbor.

DAVY ROTHBART (The Lady with the Mannequin Arm) is the author of *The Lone Surfer of Montana, Kansas* and the creator of *Found* magazine.

Jonathan Lethem (Call Waiting) is the author of *The Fortress of Solitude*. He lives in Brooklyn.

T Cooper's (Basic Rules for Handling Your Shotgun) debut novel *Some of the Parts* was a selection of the Barnes & Noble Discover Great New Writers program and Quality Paperback Book Club. T is a two-time fellow of The MacDowell Colony, and a finalist for the 2004 Koret Young Writer on Jewish Themes award, as well as editor and publisher of the Firecracker Alternative Book Award-winning 'zine "The Fish Tank."

Monica Drake (Gymkhana) is a writer and book critic living in Portland, Oregon.

Aimee Bender (Night Trilogy) is the author of *The Girl in the Flammable Skirt* and *An Invisible Sign of My Own*. Her short fiction has been published in *Harper's*, *Granta*, *Tin House*, *The Paris Review*, and more. She lives in L.A.. and teaches at USC.

Jeff Johnson (Pre-Supper Clubbing) is a regular contributor to mcsweeneys.net and a music editor at *Jane* magazine.

James Tate (Suite 1306) won the Pulitzer Prize and the William Carlos Williams Award for his *Selected Poems* in 1991. His latest book is *Return to the City of White Donkeys*.

Lucy Thomas (It's Not Black; It's Always Darker Than That) is not the real name of a bestselling author living in San Francisco.

THORN KIEF HILLSBERY (What We Do is Secret) is the author of *War Boy*.

HEIDI JULAVITS (The MacMillan Hair) is the author of *The Mineral Palace* and *The Effects of Living Backwards*.

MICHELLE TEA (Fourteenth Street) is the award-winning author of *Valencia*, *The Chelsea Whistle*, *The Beautiful*, and *Rent Girl*.

DAN KENNEDY (Tonight the Muse Is In a Popular Suburban Steakhouse Franchise) is the author of *Loser Goes First*.

STACEY RICHTER (A Case Study of Emergency Room Procedure and Risk Management by Hospital Staff Members in the Urban Facility) lives in Tuscon, Arizona. She is the author of *My Date with Satan*. Her stories have been widely anthologized and have won many prizes, including three Pushcart Prizes and the National Magazine Award.

MARSHALL MOORE (The Right Way to Eat a Bagel) is the author of *The Concrete Sky* and *Black Shapes in a Darkened Room* (Suspect Thoughts). He sometimes works as a sign language interpreter.

## About the Editor

KEVIN SAMPSELL is the publisher of the influential Portland, Oregon micro-press, Future Tense Books, which he started in 1990. He is the author of many small books including *A Common Pornography* and a collection of stories, *Beautiful Blemish* (Word Riot Press). His fiction has appeared in numerous journals including *Bridge*, *3rd Bed*, *Little Engines*, and *J&L Illustrated*, as well as on McSweeney's, Pindeldyboz, Identity Theory, Web Del Sol web sites, among others. He also performs in the spoken word group Haiku Inferno, writes book reviews for several newspapers, and works as an events coordinator for Powell's Books.

## Acknowledgments

The editor wishes to thank the following for their help and support: Nina Collins, David McCormick, Frayn Masters, Paul Ash, Mykle Hansen, Jemiah Jefferson, Mike Daily, Ritah Parrish, Zoe Trope, Reuben Nisenfeld, Jennifer Joseph, and Zacharath.

All the stories in this collection are previously unpublished in book form except the following which are used with permission:

Jonathan Ames' "Everybody Dies in Memphis" first appeared in *New York Press*.

Jonathan Lethem's "Call Waiting" first appeared in *Exquisite Corpse*.

Davy Rothbart's "The Lady with the Mannequin Arm" first appeared online at Other People's Stories.

James Tate's "Suite 1306" first appeared in *Dreams of a Robot Dancing Bee* (Verse Books).

Heidi Julavits's "The MacMillan Hair" first appeared in *Columbia.*

Stacey Richter's "A Case Study…" first appeared in *Fairy Tale Review*.